UNSIGNED AVENGER

When Will Cord is shot dead for the brutal killing of Ali Toombs, Joe Hayes and his two sons know the real killer is still at large . . . Could it be Cole Sanderson — a newcomer to Consolation? Saloon girl Maggie Brown knows he's not who he says he is. Or could it be Lew Rosen, editor of the *Gazette*, who suspects the Hayes brothers? Fear and suspicion spread like a prairie fire — is anyone safe from accusation and violence?

JOHN DAVAGE

UNSIGNED AVENGER

Complete and Unabridged

LINFORD
Leicester

First published in Great Britain in 2010 by
Robert Hale Limited, London

First Linford Edition
published 2011
by arrangement with
Robert Hale Limited, London

British Library CIP Data

Davage, John.
 Unsigned avenger. - -
 (Linford western library)
 1. Murder- -Investigation- -Fiction.
 2. Western stories.
 3. Large type books.
 I. Title II. Series
 823.9′2–dc22

 ISBN 978–1–44480–624–3

Published by
F. A. Thorpe (Publishing)
Anstey, Leicestershire

Set by Words & Graphics Ltd.
Anstey, Leicestershire
Printed and bound in Great Britain by
T. J. International Ltd., Padstow, Cornwall

This book is printed on acid-free paper

Prologue

Luther Hickson came through the batwing doors of the Horseshoe saloon like a crazed coyote. His weak, watery eyes blinked in the sudden light. His arthritic fingers curled around the double-barrelled shotgun that hung by his side, and his sun-bronzed face was a mask of hatred.

His eyes searched the room. 'Where is he?' he yelled. 'Where's Will Cord?'

Every head turned in his direction. The man playing the honky-tonk piano stopped mid-tune and the room was suddenly silent. A drifting haze of smoke hovered over the occupants of the bar area and above the three tables of poker players. At one of the tables, a young man pushed back his chair and half-stood.

Will Cord's hand hovered over the .45 strapped to his right thigh.

Luther's eyes found him. 'Child-killer!' he said, his voice cracking with emotion. 'Ali were no-but a child, Cord, and you killed her! But only after you took your filthy pleasure of her!'

Will Cord swallowed, but there was no spittle in his suddenly dry mouth. His baby-blue eyes narrowed under the fringe of ginger hair. How dangerous was the old-timer? Could those gnarled fingers hold a shotgun steady enough to find a target?

'You're crazy, Luther!' he said. 'I never touched your girl!'

Except, of course, Ali hadn't been 'Luther's girl'. No kin at all in fact, just a stray taken in after her folks had died. And as everyone in town knew, little more than a slave in the Hickson household. Given the dirtiest jobs, fed scraps, clothed in little more than rags and cast-offs. Even so, the girl was dead and Luther was looking for revenge, no doubt nettled by the loss of a skivvy, and fired up with drink.

'Go for your gun, you young

bastard!' Luther snarled, His whole body was shaking with rage. 'Go for it!' Not yet fifty, Luther looked twenty years older. He peered at Will through myopic eyes, clouded by the long-term effects of hard liquor. His head was almost bald, and grey stubble covered his chin. He carried a permanent stoop and walked with a lopsided gait.

'*Wait!*'

The voice came from the balcony which ran around one side of the room. A man moved purposefully to the head of the stairs and walked down. He was in his fifties, tall and powerfully built. He had a head of shining black hair, just beginning to grey at the temples, and a neatly trimmed goatee. He wore a white shirt, dove-grey vest and black pin-striped trousers. These were tucked into hand-tooled leather boots which had been polished to a high shine. An expensive-looking timepiece was tucked into his vest.

He made a beeline for Luther Hickson, but at a leisurely pace, assured

3

and at ease in his manner. Luther stared at him, and for the first time since entering the saloon, he seemed confused. The man said two words into Luther's left ear.

'*Not here.*'

Only Luther heard the words, but they were enough to make him look at the speaker with a puzzled expression. He opened his mouth to speak, but the older man put a hand across it and whispered another word into Luther's ear.

'*Later.*'

Again, only Luther heard it.

After a moment, he began to walk away, his stoop even more pronounced than usual. All eyes watched him as he sloped out of the saloon like a kicked cur. At the batwings, he turned and looked back at Will Cord.

'It ain't over,' he croaked, before disappearing into the darkness of the January night.

One man had watched the proceedings with the cool detachment of the experienced newspaperman. Lew Rosen, forty-five years old and proprietor, editor and printer of the *Consolation Gazette* — as yet, only a two-page news sheet, but improving by every issue in Lew's biased opinion — was sitting at his usual table in the corner of the room. He had looked up from his game of solitaire to witness the little drama that had been played out before him. It had sparked additional interest from the moment the nattily dressed figure of Joe Hayes had intervened, sending Luther away with his tail between his legs.

Now what was all that about? Lew hadn't heard what Joe had whispered into Luther's ear, couldn't begin to guess, but it had been powerful persuasive.

It was all *very* interesting, Lew decided.

★   ★   ★

Later that evening, just before eight o'clock, Will Cord made his way from the saloon and turned into the alleyway that led between Esau Parker's livery stables and Joe Caton's dry goods store. He was a trifle unsteady on his feet, having had more than his usual intake of alcohol after the unsettling events of the early evening. What had that been all about? Crazy old fool! What in hell was Luther thinking of? Kill Ali Toombs? Why, he hardly knew the girl. He'd heard about her death, who hadn't? but it had nothing to do with him.

Besides, Will had other things on his mind. Something he had to do. It wasn't a question of duty, or even of 'doing the right thing'. He had made his mind up, and tomorrow he would take the first steps to put the situation right.

He would ask Jane to marry him. Sure he would. Wasn't she the prettiest girl he'd ever seen? Wasn't she the best thing that had ever happened to him? Right! So he would ask her first thing tomorrow.

But there was to be no tomorrow for Will Cord . . .

The shot came out of the darkness of the alleyway before he had taken half-a-dozen steps. The slug caught him in the middle of his chest and hurled him off his feet. He was dead before he hit the alleyway dirt, his eyes glazing to a fixed stare.

Both Esau Parker and Joe Caton heard the shot and, after taking care to assure themselves that they themselves wouldn't become targets of some trigger-happy gunman, emerged cautiously into the alleyway. They saw the crumpled shape on the ground and moved slowly towards it from opposite directions.

'It's Will Cord,' Esau announced, as he bent over the body.

'Is he dead?' Joe asked.

'Dead as hell,' Esau told him.

'I'll get the sheriff,' Joe said.

'And I'll get Ed Hawker,' Esau said. 'He ain't in need of no doc, just an undertaker.'

After the two men disappeared out of the alleyway, a figure emerged from the

7

shadows. It moved silently across to Will Cord's body and slipped two items into the pocket of the dead man's buckskin jacket.

★ ★ ★

Once the identity of the body had been verified, and the fact that he'd been the victim of a shotgun killing, there was no doubt about whose hands had held the weapon. There had been plenty of witnesses of the altercation in the saloon earlier. But there was no *proof* that Luther Hickson had fired the fatal shot that ended the life of Will Cord. And Luther refused to say anything. Fact was, he seemed confused about the whole business.

'Shock,' people said. 'Poor old Luther! Not loco, but near to it after that girl's horrible death. 'Course he did the killin'!'

It was a time when folks settled their own difficulties, meted out their own interpretation of justice. And once an oval tin-plate locket and a letter scribbled in what could have been Ali's childish handwriting had been discovered in the pocket of Will Cord's jacket, all doubts had melted away. The locket was one that Ali had always worn around her neck. The letter indicated that she was carrying Will's baby and that she planned to make this known to everybody unless he upped and married her.

So, people said, Luther had simply avenged Ali's death. Case closed.

★　★　★

The date was 15 January, 1867. The place was Consolation Township, in the west of Arizona. A one-horse town surrounded by a handful of homesteads and one large ranch. It boasted a couple of stores, a saloon, a boarding house and a low-roofed adobe sheriff's office, and not much more.

By 1886 it would be bigger, but still hardly a thriving little centre of commerce. The railroad had passed it by, no gold or silver had been discovered in the surrounding hills. But suddenly someone seemed to want to reawaken interest in something that certain townspeople had hoped was long since forgotten.

1

Cole Sanderson rode his sorrel into Consolation on a warm April afternoon. He was thirty years old, a tall, lean man with grey eyes that mirrored much of the grief and hardship that life had thrown him. His features were sun-bronzed and knife-blade thin, and his black, flat-crowned sombrero etched shadows across his face as he stared down the town's main street.

There was a schoolhouse at the far end of the town, and a white-painted wooden church. Nearer was a two-storey hotel, two saloons, one with the sign Roxy's Palace over its boardwalk, the other, a smaller building announcing itself as the Horseshoe. Cole also noted a dry goods store, a livery, a newspaper office, a barbershop, and a low-roofed sheriff's office.

It was mid-afternoon and a couple of

old-timers sat in high-backed chairs on the boardwalk outside the barbershop, having found some shade. A swamper pushed a besom along the boardwalk outside Roxy's Palace, and a couple of horses were drooping in the heat at the hitching rail outside the Horseshoe. Nothing else moved.

Cole left his horse at the livery, gathered up his saddle-bags and the Winchester, and walked to the hotel. The clerk at the desk looked up. At his first glance of Cole, fear momentarily flickered across the man's eyes before he opened his mouth to speak.

'Mornin', sir,' he said. He stood with his arms crossed, his fingers playing with the armbands on his shirtsleeves. He was a skinny guy in his middle forties, with a drooping black moustache and hair plastered to his scalp by over-zealous use of goose-grease.

'Need a room,' Cole said.

'Yessir.' The clerk turned and took a key from one of the cubby-holes behind him. 'Room twenty, top floor. How long you planning to stay?'

'Ain't decided,' Cole told him. He took the key and made for the stairs.

He'd told the truth. He *hadn't* decided. Why had he come here? A score to be settled? A wrong to be righted? Maybe, but after all this time . . . He pushed the thoughts from his mind. Consolation held no pleasant memories for him, but lately no place satisfied him for long, so what did it matter? Nothing mattered. 'Just keep movin' on,' that's what he told himself.

★   ★   ★

The stranger to town had been observed by the proprietor of the *Consolation Gazette*. Lew Rosen had been looking out of his office window and his sharp eye had taken in the .45 in the low-slung leather holster strapped to the stranger's waist, and the Winchester in its scabbard. Lew had felt an uneasy stirring in the pit of his stomach, and he didn't put it down to the beef dinner he'd downed at Nettie Garland's eating-house less than an hour earlier. Nossir, as a news-paperman and a resident of Consolation for some thirty years, Lew reckoned he could smell trouble at first glance. And to his eye, every inch of the stranger spelled trouble.

'I know a gunslinger when I see one,' he muttered to himself.

In an upstairs room in Roxy's Palace, Wes Hayes was putting on his pants. The girl in the bed watched him covertly with barely concealed hatred, even though only minutes before she had been whispering words of endear-ment and encouragement into his ear as he had lain on top of her. Words on which she had almost choked, but which she knew he expected to hear.

'Same time tomorrow, Maggie,' Wes Hayes said.

'Sure, Wes,' Maggie replied. She forced a smile. 'I'll look forward to it.'

He turned and grinned at her. ''Course you will, girl.'

Wes Hayes was forty-two years old.

His wife, Mary, had died two years ago, but he had been availing himself of the pleasures of Roxy's Palace girls for much longer than that. And before Roxy had opened her saloon, there had been a string of girls at the Horseshoe ready and willing to accommodate the youngest son of Consolation's richest and most powerful man.

Maggie had been told all this by Roxy soon after she had come to work at Roxy's Palace, and after Wes had informed Roxy that he wanted Maggie to be his exclusively, and not available to other customers. A sum of money had exchanged hands before Roxy had agreed to this arrangement, a little of which had been passed to Maggie.

Roxy had also warned Maggie about Wes Hayes's explosive temper.

'Sweet-talk him, and you'll be OK,' Roxy had said. 'Make him mad, and you'll find out just what a mean critter he can be.'

Now, Wes strapped on his gunbelt then pushed a hand through his shock of prematurely grey hair.

'You're a strange one, Maggie Brown,' he said. 'Never sure what you're thinkin'. Never sure what's goin' on in that head of yours.'

Which is just as well, Maggie thought. She pushed herself up in the bed, holding the covers across her naked breasts. 'Nothin's goin' on, Wes,' she said. 'Too much thinkin' is bad for a person, I always say.'

He looked piercingly at her for a moment, then relaxed and laughed. 'Maybe you're right.'

When he had gone, she threw back the bed covers and walked naked across the room. 'Bastard!' she muttered, grabbing her clothes from the hurriedly discarded pile on the chair. 'Filthy low-life!'

* * *

Ten minutes later, having pushed a comb through her red hair and put fresh paint on her face, Maggie descended the stairs into the saloon. Wes Hayes was just leaving the premises, presumably having had his usual post-coital shot of whiskey to restore his strength.

Maggie looked across the room — and got a shock.

There was a man sitting at the bar, a stranger to Consolation but not to her. Where had she seen him before? Maggie had been in Consolation only a few months. Prior to that there had been a succession of towns, both small and large, each one another step towards Consolation, her intended target. Each saloon another notch on her belt of experience. Now, aged nineteen, she was ready for most things life could throw at her.

The man was talking to Roxy, whose corpulent figure was leaning against the other side of the bar, her eyes flashing under her fringe of expertly dyed corn-coloured hair, her powdered breasts bulging over the top of her dress.

'That was Wes Hayes,' Maggie heard

Roxy say. 'Big man in this town. Best to keep on the right side of him, mister.'

The man said something, to which Roxy gave one of her belly laughs.

'Oh, sure!' she said. 'He's been availin' himself of Roxy's comforts for many a year now. Leastwise, he was until he discovered young Maggie Brown over there. Now I'm on the shelf! Used goods!' She gave another good-natured belly laugh. 'Suits me fine. I'm gettin' a tad too old for the kind of high jinks Mister Wes Hayes likes goin' in for.'

At the mention of Maggie's name, the man turned and looked across at her. And Maggie saw the unmistakable flash of recognition in his eyes.

She held her breath. Was he going to say something? Something like, 'She wasn't Maggie *Brown* when I knew her.' But no, he just tipped his hat, nodded in her direction, then turned back to Roxy.

Maggie breathed easily again.

She crossed the room and went to sit

at a table with two of the other saloon girls. She joined in the desultory conversation for the next few minutes, but her mind was busy. The stranger had definitely recognized her from somewhere, so why hadn't he said anything? Maybe because, like her, he had his reasons for not wanting his own identity known.

*　*　*

Lew Rosen frowned as he saw the man coming towards him across the street. He had no desire to meet Wes Hayes this afternoon, but the encounter was clearly unavoidable. Indeed, Wes's tall, muscular figure was bearing down on him rapidly, and the man had a purposeful look in his eye.

'Aft'noon, Lew,' Wes said, as the two men met on the boardwalk outside the offices of the *Consolation Herald*. The smile pasted on Wes's face was deceiving. There was certainly no warmth in it.

'Aft'noon, Wes,' Lew replied.

'Now tell me, Lew,' Wes said, 'just what is it you've got against me? What's a-promptin' you to write those nasty things about me in that paper of yours? Oh, sure, I know you don't 'xactly mention my *name*, but everybody in town knows it's me your referrin' to.'

Lew took a cheroot from the case in his waistcoat pocket and lit it, his eyes never leaving Wes's face. At last he said, 'I just try to write the truth, Wes. And it's true that it ain't healthy for one family to have so much say-so in a town this size. For one family to own nearly every damn thing, including the bank, kinda makes for a monopoly situation, and that ain't good for anybody. 'Cept maybe you and your brother.'

'Now, Lew — ' began Wes, an edge to his voice.

'And now that brother of yours is tryin' to foreclose on Vince Chessman's mortgage so that you and your family can get your hands on Vince's dry goods store,' Lew went on, trying to ignore the dangerous look in Wes's eye.

'How Harry runs the bank is nothing to do with me,' Wes said. 'And nothin' to do with you and your paper.' He pushed his face inches from Lew's nose and lowered his voice. 'Just watch what you're writin' about my family in future, Rosen, else you're gonna find you ain't got no paper to write in, and no machines for all that other stuff you print.'

'What you sayin', Wes? That 'accidents' happen around here? Well, everybody knows that. Ain't that how you got most of the land around here? Mysterious fires destroyin' homesteads and burnin' crops, afore you or Harry moved in an' bought up what was left?'

'Why, you — !'

'Ease off, Wes,' Lew said. 'There are a few things I *could* tell about you and your brother. Not in my paper, maybe, 'cause I ain't aimin' to attract a libel suit, but there are other ways.'

With that, Lew pushed past Wes and headed towards Roxy's Palace.

* * *

Wes stared after him, swearing softly. Just what was Lew Rosen getting at? *A few things I could tell about you and your brother.* Wes didn't like the sound of that. Maybe it was time to do something about Lew Rosen and his damn paper. He'd been a thorn in the side of the Hayes family for too long.

2

The next day, Cole rode a half-familiar trail out to the Circle H spread, but did not venture anywhere near the house, the bunkhouses or the corral. As he stood, carefully concealed on the fringe of the pine forest looking down into the valley, memories flooded back, some good, some bad, but he pushed them from his mind. He had no clear idea of his intentions, or even of why he'd come here. But something, some instinct, had drawn him back to this place. After a time, he turned and rode back to town.

When he got back to the livery with his horse, old Esau Parker informed him that the Circle H had about twenty cowpunchers working there.

'Leastways,' Esau said, 'that's what Wes Hayes calls 'em. Half of 'em look more like gunslingers to me. They come into town, rowdyin' the place up and shootin' their mouths off. Best to stay clear of 'em, if'n yuh ask me.'

'Is old man Hayes still alive?' Cole asked.

Esau looked surprised. 'Yuh know Joe Hayes?'

Cole made no reply.

'Well, old Joe is still alive — just,' Esau said. 'They say he's a dyin' man, though.'

That evening, after eating at the hotel, Cole went across to Roxy's Palace. The barkeep served him a beer and Cole took himself off to a quiet corner table. He built himself a smoke, then opened up a copy of last week's *Consolation Gazette*. After a few minutes of reading Lew Rosen's editorial attacking monopoly interests in the town, Cole became aware of a ruckus at the bar.

He looked up to see the girl they called Maggie Brown wrestling with some stocky, lantern-jawed *hombre* who'd clearly had too much to drink. The man was trying to shove one hand down the front of Maggie's dress and pawing her breasts with the other. Maggie was trying, unsuccessfully, to fight him off.

For a minute or so, Cole hesitated about whether or not to interfere. Saloon girls had to accept a certain amount of horseplay, it went with the job, but this guy was getting nasty, you could see it in his face.

'Quit fightin' me, Maggie!' he was yelling.

She was backed over the edge of the bar, her red hair splayed out across the counter-top. Unable to prise the man's hands away from the front of her dress, she attacked his face, drawing three lines of blood down one cheek with her painted fingernails.

'Bitch!' the man shouted, and cuffed her across the mouth.

It was enough for Cole. He rose rapidly to his feet and strode across. In one swift movement he yanked the man away from the girl by his shoulders and shoved him backwards against a table covered with empty glasses. The table gave under the man's weight, and he hit the floor accompanied by a crash of splintered wood and broken glass.

'You OK?' Cole asked the girl.

Maggie rubbed the fast-growing swelling under her left eye and nodded. 'Yeah, thanks,' she said. 'But you've made yourself a powerful enemy, mister.'

There was no time for Cole to answer as the other man was on his feet and coming towards him, arms swinging, his broad body in a half-crouch. Cole twisted sideways in the nick of time, and unleashed a body blow that sank into the man's stomach, knocking the breath out of him. The man rocked for a moment, then his knees buckled and he slipped to the floor again.

He lay there for several seconds, gaining his breath, then he let his gaze drift away from Cole's face and beyond. It was an old trick, hoping to divert Cole's attention long enough to gain an advantage on the draw. Cole didn't fall for it.

As the other man drew, Cole's .45 Peacemaker seemed to leap from its holster and into his hand as if by magic. The shot whipped the gun from the other man's hand and blood erupted between his fingers.

Cole re-holstered his .45 and waited.

The other man struggled to his feet, nursing his injured hand, his eyes blazing. Another *hombre*, one of the man's pals, picked up his friend's gun and put it back in its holster.

'Leave it, Jud,' he said. 'There'll be another time to settle this with the sonofabitch.'

'There sure will,' the man called Jud said, his eyes not leaving Cole's face. 'This ain't over, mister.'

Cole shrugged and watched the two men leave.

'Who were they?' he asked Maggie, after they had gone.

'The man who tried to shoot you is Jud Grey, Wes Hayes's foreman,' she told him. 'The other one is Jim Ellis, one of the hands at the Circle H. You'd better watch your back from now on.' She gave him a long, knowing look, then added, 'But I guess you're used to doin' that.'

He stared at her silently for several seconds, then he said, 'I was, but that was some time ago. Guess I'll have to sharpen up again.'

'Guess you will,' she said.

She turned and walked towards the stairs, heading for her room. As she did so, Roxy Wells came through a doorway behind the bar.

The saloon owner had been taking a nap in the little office, back of the bar. Had anyone asked her if she'd been sleeping, she'd have hotly denied it, unwilling to accept that these days she got tired more easily and that a sixty-year-old woman needed the occasional daytime nap. Roxy was fighting a losing battle against her age, and secretly admitted this to herself. Certainly each time she looked at the pretty Maggie Brown she had to concede that maybe she'd lost *some* of her youthful charms.

'What's all the ruckus?' she asked the barkeep. 'I heard shootin'.'

The barkeep gave her a brief explanation, and her eyes widened. 'Jud Grey!' she said. She looked across at Cole.

'I know,' he said, before she could speak. 'I'll need to watch my back.'

She grinned. 'You sure will, mister,' she said.

★   ★   ★

The following day, Harry Hayes got a chilling reminder of something he had hoped was dead and buried long ago. An envelope was on his desk at the bank when he arrived that morning. His name was written on the front.

Harry opened it and took out a single sheet of paper. As he read the words on it, the colour drained from his normally heavily flushed face.

Ali Toombs — I know the truth. It's time others did too.

Harry sank into his office chair, his heartbeat quickening and a cold sweat breaking out on his forehead. He pulled open a desk drawer and took out the small bottle containing pills Doc Tully had prescribed him. He shook two from the bottle and shoved them in his mouth.

'Cy!' he yelled. 'Get in here!'

Cy Carter, the youngest bank teller, came into Harry's office a moment later. 'Yessir, Mister Hayes?' he said.

'This letter,' Harry said. 'How'd it get here?'

'Found it pushed under the door when I got here this mornin',' Cy said.

Harry stared at the envelope again. 'Did you see who delivered it? Anybody walkin' away from the bank?'

'Nossir, Mr Hayes,' Cy said.

'All right.' Harry waved the young man away. 'I have to go out. I'll be back in an hour or so.'

He stuffed the letter and envelope into his jacket pocket, picked up his hat and stuck it on his balding head, then headed for the back door of the bank.

'Gotta see Wes,' he muttered to himself, as he pulled his overweight frame onto the buggy tethered at the rear of the building. 'Gotta see Wes.'

An hour later, he had thrust the anonymous note into his brother's hand and was watching Wes's face closely. A steely look came into Wes Hayes's eyes as he stared at the sheet of paper.

'What's it mean, Wes?' Harry asked, wiping the sweat from his brow with a red handkerchief. 'How come, after all this time — '

'How'n hell do I know?' Wes barked.

They were in Wes's study at the Circle H ranch house. It was a large room with heavy furniture and oak-panelled walls. Wes's desk was twice the size of the one Harry occupied at the bank. Papers were strewn across it, and a cigar box lay open at one side. Wes sat in a leather-backed swivel chair, a cigar moving between his teeth as he spoke.

'Lew Rosen,' he said slowly. He chewed on his cigar for a moment, then went on. 'What was it he said to me the other day? There were *other ways* besides his damned newspaper to tell folks about things you and me wouldn't partic'ly want talked about. But this ain't tellin' other people, this is just meant to scare the hell out of you, Harry.'

'Well, it sure as hell's workin',' Harry said. 'But why now, after all this time?'

'Dunno,' Wes said. 'He was kinda riled about you foreclosin' on Vince Chessman's mortgage. Coulda been that which prompted him. Can't think of nothin' else.'

'But we agreed it was time to squeeze Vince out of the dry goods store, Wes,' Harry said. 'You told me — '

'Yes, dammit, I know what I told you!' Wes growled. 'And nothin's changed. We go ahead. I'll talk to Rosen. Leave it with me, Harry, and get back to the bank.' He shook his head. 'You sure as hell scare easy these days, Brother. You used to be the strong one, remember? Nobody frightened Harry

Hayes: *he* scared *them*. Whatever happened to that guy, Harry?'

Harry mopped the sweat from his forehead and looked away. 'Guess I've changed, Wes,' he said.

'Ain't that the truth,' Wes said. He pushed the note and the envelope into a desk drawer.

'Ain't gonna look good to Coleen, when she gets here, if she gets to see one of these notes afore I do,' Harry said. 'Could put the weddin' in jeopardy. She knows nothin' about my — er — past life.'

'We'll do somethin' about the damn notes afore she gets here,' Wes told him.

'She's comin' next week,' Harry told him. 'She'll be stayin' at the hotel. Weddin's planned for next month, Wes. There ain't much time.' He took a handkerchief from his pocket and mopped his brow.

'Quit fussin',' Wes said. 'It'll be all right. Coleen ain't gonna find out anythin'.'

In fact, Wes was more worried than

he sounded. Harry's forthcoming wedding to a rich widow from the East was something he highly approved of, if only so that the Hayes family could get their hands on her money. From what his brother had told him, she was close to being a millionairess. Love-sick Harry may not have considered that important when he'd met and wooed Mrs Coleen Milton on his last trip to Chicago, but Wes had immediately realized the potential of the situation. So for this particular skeleton from the past to suddenly come out of the cupboard was the last thing he wanted.

There was a shuffling sound in the passage outside. A moment later, old Joe Hayes appeared in the doorway. He was breathing heavily and leaning on a polished walking stick.

'Hello, Pa,' Harry said. 'I — '

'Harry had some papers for me to sign, Pa,' Wes said, throwing a warning glance at his brother. 'Was there somethin' you wanted?'

Joe Hayes moved slowly across the

room and sat himself down in an armchair next to the window. His once-shining black hair was now white, and the neatly trimmed goatee now just a straggly attachment to his ever-thinning face. His hooded eyes were the eyes of a dying man, and when he spoke his voice was little more than a croak.

'Saw you arrive, Harry,' he said. 'Looked like you'd seen a ghost. Somethin' wrong?'

Harry glanced at his brother, then said, 'Nothin', Pa. Just bank business. You know how it is.'

'That's just it, I don't know anythin' that's goin' on any more. You two tell me nothin'.' The old man turned and stared out of the window. 'I used to run this place nigh on single-handed. Knew every damn thing that happened within a radius of fifty mile and nipped problems in the bud afore they got outa hand. 'Specially with you two hell-raisers causin' trouble wherever you went.'

'That was a long time ago, Pa,' Harry

said. 'Things are different now.'

Joe Hayes turned back and gave his oldest son a worried stare. 'Are they? I hope you're right, Harry. I'm gettin' too old to clear up after your messes.'

'I — I gotta get back to the bank,' Harry said.

'Sure, Harry,' Wes said, a reassuring smile on his face, mostly for his father's benefit. 'You can leave that other matter with me. I'll handle it. So long.'

Harry left the room in a hurry. When he'd gone, Joe Hayes looked across at Wes.

'What's all this about Jud and some fight in Roxy's Palace? I hear he tried to draw against some gunslinger.'

'Aw, it was nothin', Pa,' Wes said. 'Seems he got a bit carried away with one of the saloon girls and this stranger decided to interfere. Nothin' I can't deal with.'

'Jud's a hothead and a fool,' Joe said. He shook his head sadly. 'Wes, I don't like some of these fellas you hire. Think I don't know gunslingers when I see

36

them? The men I used to employ — '

'Times have changed, Pa,' Wes cut in, an edge coming into his voice. 'It ain't easy runnin' things nowadays, keepin' control. But we look after our own at Circle H, so I'll put the stranger right, don't worry.'

But not until I've dealt with Lew Rosen, he thought.

3

Cole was eating breakfast in the hotel dining-room when he had a visitor. He looked up at the sound of his name.

'Sanderson?'

Sheriff Warren Speer was twenty-eight years old, lean and lanky, with a nose shaped like a buzzard's beak. He had been sheriff in Consolation for two years, elected to the post just a month after marrying Wes Hayes's daughter Lucy. Before that, he'd been just another cowpuncher on the Circle H ranch.

He'd heard about the fight between Sanderson and Jud Grey late the previous evening, and had guessed news of it would have got to Wes Hayes by now. He also knew that Wes would expect him to do something about it, hence the reason for his visit to the hotel.

Cole Sanderson nodded in answer to Warren's question, but continued to eat his ham and eggs.

'You plannin' on stayin' long in Consolation?' Warren asked.

'Ain't decided,' Cole said.

'Just want you to know Consolation ain't no place for gunslingers, if'n that's what you are,' Warren said.

'From what I hear, you already have more than your share workin' at the Circle H,' Cole said.

Warren's eyes narrowed. 'Just stay out of trouble, mister, or you'll be seein' the inside of my gaol. We don't take kindly to folks interferin' in our business.'

'Seems to me it was the other *hombre* doin' the interferin' — with a lady,' Cole said.

'Horseplay, nothin' more,' Warren said. 'Maggie's used to a bit of horseplay.'

'Didn't look that way to me.' Cole poured himself more coffee. 'And I don't like to see a man hit a woman.'

39

Warren shifted uncomfortably on his feet and ran his hat brim through his fingers. 'Maggie can take care of herself. Next time, leave things be. No more gunplay.'

Cole pushed his plate away and stared coolly at the sheriff. 'Ain't makin' no promises,' he said.

Both men were silent for a long minute, then Warren turned and walked from the room.

He went back to his office, pulled a wad of old law dodgers from his desk drawer, and began to sift through the stained and dog-eared sheets. Ten minutes later, he let out an exclamation of triumph.

'Ha! So, that's who you are, mister,' he said to himself. 'Cole Chance, one-time member of the Brennan Gang. Well, whaddaya know!'

* * *

Maggie Brown was soaking in a tub at the saloon. She lay back in the water,

40

her face a picture of concentration. The idea that had come to her after first seeing Cole Sanderson was taking shape in her mind, encouraged by the way he'd come to her rescue the previous day.

She'd finally remembered where she had seen him before. It had been four years ago, in Buckland, a small border town where she'd found a job in one of the two saloons. She'd known nothing about him, but somebody — a stranger passing through — had told her that Cole Sanderson was actually the gunslinger, Cole Chance, onetime member of the notorious Brennan Gang.

One evening in the saloon, after having had what was probably a few drinks too many, she had been emboldened enough to address him as 'Mr Chance'. The look in his eyes and the way he had whipped round to face her was enough to make her stomach do a somersault, and for her glass to slip through her fingers and smash on the floor.

'Sanderson's the name, lady,' he had said softly. 'Remember that.'

His visits to the saloon had been infrequent before, but they had dried up completely after that. She learned from local people that Cole Sanderson had a small farm about twenty miles outside town, and that he was married and had a small child just a few months old. It seemed the onetime gunslinger was trying to leave his old life behind him and start afresh.

A few months later, Maggie had moved on, eventually arriving in Consolation and getting a job at Roxy's. She had heard nothing and had thought nothing of Cole Sanderson-Chance until he had turned up in the town a couple of days ago.

Now, as she soaped her shoulders and the tops of her breasts in a leisurely fashion, she was beginning to think his presence here could prove useful to her. Clearly he was no small-time farmer any more, and his eyes spoke of a recent tragedy. But why was he here?

Roxy, who'd had a conversation with him after the previous night's ruckus, seemed to think he knew, or had once known, the Hayes family, but that they were no particular friends of his. But were they his reason for picking Consolation as a destination? Or was it simply a coincidence?

Either way, Maggie decided, a man who was prepared to defend a lady's honour once, might be persuaded to do it again. Maybe she could engineer a confrontation with Wes or Harry Hayes when Cole was around, and maybe with more fatal results.

As she pictured the scenario in her head, a smile spread slowly across her face.

* * *

Nettie Garland's eating-house was reckoned to serve the best food in town, which was why Lew Rosen and Max Prentiss were tucking into a second helping of some of Nettie's pancakes. Vince Chessman, the third man at the table, seemed to have little appetite and was watching the other two morosely.

After a minute or two, Lew wiped his mouth with the back of his hand and sat back in his chair. He pulled a narrow sheet of printed paper from his pocket and put it on the table.

'What's that?' Max asked. He was the town's corn merchant, a short, spare man with a shiny bald head.

'A proof copy of my editorial for Friday's *Gazette*,' Lew informed him. 'Thought you might want to see it.'

He turned the sheet of paper round so that both men could read it. After they had finished. Max whistled.

'Strong stuff,' he said. 'Harry Hayes ain't gonna like that.'

'Says nothin' about Harry Hayes, as far as I can see,' Lew said.

'No, but people ain't fools, Lew,' Vince said. 'Not when you write '*one man's unhealthy control of the town's finances, and the decisions taken for the so-called good of the town*'. With Harry Hayes bein' mayor *and* owner of the bank, it's obvious who you're talkin' about, ain't it?'

'Vince is right,' Nettie said. She had come up behind them and had overheard the conversation. 'You're playing with fire, Lew.'

Lew turned and looked up .into Nettie's melon-shaped face. He put an arm half-way round her waist — it was as far as he could reach, Nettie being a lady of ample proportions.

'Don't worry about me, Nettie,' he said. 'It's Vince here with the most pressin' problem. Harry Hayes is about to foreclose on his mortgage, forcin' him into bankruptcy.' He snorted. 'Just another business for the Hayes brothers to scoop up at a chicken-feed price.' He looked at the corn merchant. 'You'll be next, Max, mark my words, then Roxy's saloon'll be in their line of fire.'

They were silent for some minutes before Max spoke.

'Just who's this stranger stayin' at

Harry Hayes's hotel? I heared tell he shot Jud Grey's gun right out of his hand. Some gunslinger or other?'

'Don't know,' Lew said, 'but I aim to find out as soon as we're finished here. Plan to go across to the hotel and have a word with him, that's if he'll talk to me. Might have a word with Roxy, too. Seems she had some talk with him and maybe knows somethin'.'

★ ★ ★

At Roxy's Palace, Maggie breathed easy as Wes Hayes rolled off her on to the other side of her bed. She heard his snort of exasperation and hesitated before speaking.

'Somethin' wrong, Wes?' she said. 'Not like you to be unable to — '

'Yeah, yeah, all right, girl!' Wes snapped, embarrassed by his inability to perform.

'Somethin' on your mind?' Maggie asked. Secretly, she was delighted by the reprieve, and the possibility that all was not well in the life of Wes Hayes.

He yanked back the bedcovers and started to dress. Truth was, he was more worried by that anonymous note than he'd let on to his brother. Was it the work of Lew Rosen? He couldn't imagine who else could have written it. There weren't that many people left in the town who had been around at the time of Ali Toombs's death.

It had been years since he'd given even a passing thought to all that . . . business. Now, and when he'd been sprawled on top of Maggie, a vivid picture had entered his head. A picture of a scrawny girl, dressed in rags — well, mostly undressed — lying bleeding on the ground in the depths of the pine forest at the edge of the Circle H. Dead eyes staring up at him and his brother as they had scrambled, panic-stricken, into their pants.

The remembrance of those dead eyes had been enough to shrivel his manhood.

They had also been the subject of a

succession of nightmares for months after the event, even after Joe Hayes had managed to persuade Luther Hickson that Ali's death had been the work of Will Cord. Will was a onetime pal of theirs who had partaken in many of their hell-raising exploits until he'd taken a shine to Jane Duggan. But even after Will had been shot by a hired gun, paid for by Joe Hayes, the damned dream wouldn't go away, and Wes would wake up sweating and shaking in the night.

Now, nearly twenty years later, somebody was trying to stir up that old hornets' nest of trouble again. Why now? Was it really because the Hayes brothers were strengthening their grip on the township of Consolation, and somebody — Lew Rosen? — didn't like it? But what was the point? Nobody could prove anything after all this time.

Then Wes remembered the effect the anonymous note had had on Harry. Reduced him to a nervous wreck in minutes. Why, chances were, he'd start drinking heavily again, the way he had in the years after Ali's death. And alcohol, taken in the quantities that Harry could consume it, had a habit of loosening his tongue. Dangerously so.

Wes finished dressing and went to the window, oblivious of the fact that Maggie was watching him thoughtfully. He stared across the street at the front of the *Gazette* office. Through the half-frosted glass, he could see Lew Rosen working at the large flat-bed printing machine, no doubt preparing Friday's issue of the newspaper. What was his editorial going to say this time? More claptrap about monopoly ownership and the Hayes family?

And now the bastard was scaring the hell out of Harry with anonymous notes. Wasn't he? Who else in town would remember Ali Toombs's violent end?

Wes needed to think. Needed to plan. There was too much at stake for things to start coming apart now.

And then there was his father. Old

Joe was dying, and Wes planned to have him die in peace. Besides, he and Harry no longer needed the old man to fight their battles any more. Sure, Joe Hayes had been able to sort out most problems in the old days, but those days were long gone. Now he, Wes, was in control. Anybody needed buying off, Harry handled it. Anybody needed a spot of intimidation, Wes had the men to do it. Sure, some of those men were cold, ruthless killers, but they were the sort of men he needed to maintain the kind of authority he and Harry had in Consolation.

Wes suddenly remembered Jud Grey's skirmish with the stranger. He needed to see his son-in-law and check what Warren had done about the fracas in the saloon, if anything. Couldn't have strangers interfering in what happened in Consolation, especially when the Circle H foreman was involved.

'You OK, Wes?'

Maggie's voice awakened him from his musings, and he turned away from the window. He stared at her for a moment, then left the room without answering her.

So he didn't see the satisfied smile on Maggie's face as she slid beneath the bedcovers, hands behind her head.

4

Warren Speer looked up from his desk as Wes came into his office. His young deputy, Bud Randall, automatically rose from his chair and made for the door. One glance at Wes's sour face had been enough for Bud to beat a hasty retreat.

'Guess I'll just go out and check on a few things, Warren,' he said.

'Sure, Bud,' Warren replied, sweat already beginning to form on his forehead, the way it always did when his father-in-law came to see him.

Wes waited until Bud had shut the door before speaking. 'You done anythin' about that critter who shot up Jud Grey, Warren?'

'Sure, Wes,' Warren replied, relieved he'd been quick off the mark in going to see Cole Sanderson. 'Went and had a talk with him first thing this mornin'.

He smiled. 'Calls himself Cole Sanderson, but his real name's Cole Chance, a gunfighter.' He pulled the old law dodger from his desk drawer and laid it flat on the top for Wes to see. 'One-time member of the Brennan Gang.'

Wes stared at it for a full minute without speaking. Indeed, Warren was beginning to get nervous, wondering if he'd done something wrong by unearthing the fact that the stranger was a gunslinger.

'Chance,' Wes said eventually. 'Chance . . . Why does that name ring a bell?' He thought for a moment more, then slammed a fist down on Warren's desk, making the sheriff jump. 'Of course! Evan Chance had a homestead twenty miles outside Consolation, years ago. Got burned out in a — uh — accidental fire. He had a son. Can't remember the kid's name, but he woulda been about nine or ten years old at the time. How old's this fella?'

' 'Bout thirty, I'd guess,' Warren said.

Wes nodded. 'That works out.

Woulda been about twenty years ago when Chance and his family moved on.' Memories were surfacing in Wes's head, and he didn't like what he was remembering. For a start, had Chance and his kid been around at the time Ali Toombs had died? He had a feeling that they had.

'What d'you want me to do about this Chance fella?' Warren asked. He'd planned on letting the county marshal know he'd got a wanted man in town, albeit a man wanted by the law some seven or eight years ago. Now he wasn't so sure.

'Nothin',' Wes told him. 'Not for the moment, anyhow. I'll tell you when to make a move on him. Maybe he'll be travellin' on in a day or two.'

Something told Warren that Wes had said that more in hope than expectation. Something was telling him that Chance's presence in town was bothering Wes more than it should, something Wes needed to deal with before letting Warren take any action.

Warren watched him leave, puzzled by the turn of events. He was scared of his father-in-law, he admitted that to himself. But he also had an intense dislike of gunslingers. Many years ago, his own father had been killed by one when he'd been an innocent bystander during a bank robbery. He'd also heard something about the so-called 'accidental' crop and homestead fires of the past, but he tried not to think about them.

Warren tried hard to keep a clean town, but he found both Wes and Harry Hayes difficult to get on with. He had this ongoing inner conflict — wanting to see justice done but afraid of getting on the wrong side of his father-in-law, thus upsetting Lucy, his wife. And Lucy always tended to side with her father.

Wes also had a certain amount of financial control over Warren, having built Warren and Lucy a home at the far end of town, and by continually giving Lucy money she didn't really need. Warren would have preferred it not to be this way, but seemed unable to stop it.

He pushed the law dodger back into his desk drawer, just as Bud Randall returned.

'Everythin' OK, boss?' Bud asked.

'Sure,' Warren said with a sigh. 'Everythin's OK.'

★　★　★

Harry Hayes had abandoned his desk at the bank for the rest of the morning. Instead, he was drinking down his fourth shot of gut-rot whiskey in the Horseshoe saloon. He rarely frequented Roxy's Palace. For one thing, although Doug Jenson ran the Horseshoe, Harry and his brother owned it. And pretty soon, they would own Roxy's Palace, too.

The other reason Harry avoided the other saloon was Maggie Brown. Whenever he bumped into her, in the street or at the bank when she was paying in Roxy's takings, she gave him a look that was pure hatred. Never said anything, just looked. It unnerved him every time. Made his stomach churn. He didn't know why. What did the little cat have against him, for Cris'sakes? But somehow, he'd never got up the nerve to ask. And he'd certainly never mentioned it to Wes, whom, he knew, enjoyed the whore's company.

He'd seen her looking out of her bedroom window at the Palace about ten minutes after his brother would have left her. Seen her staring down at him as he'd sidled into the Horseshoe, hoping to be unnoticed by any passing bank client, although he didn't know why. Dammit, he could go where he liked, couldn't he? And if he wanted to get a drink or two mid-morning, so what? But she'd seen him, and it had aroused the usual stomach-churning sensation. Bitch!

Two other people had seen him enter the Horseshoe. Lew Rosen had been coming out of the Gazette office and had given him a wave. There had been a smirk on Lew's face, almost as if he'd known something was troubling Harry, dispatching him to the comforts of the Horseshoe to take his mind off his problems.

Then there'd been that stranger to town, coming out of the hotel. It was the first time Harry had seen him, but word of Jud Grey's encounter with the gunman had reached him, along with a description of the *hombre*. So Harry had no doubt who the man was who threw a glance in his direction as he came out on to the hotel boardwalk. And something in the stranger's look had sent a chill up Harry's spine.

Now, pouring himself his fifth shot of whiskey, he was too far gone to be aware of the young kid who slipped an envelope unnoticed into Harry's jacket pocket. Too slow to turn and ask him what he was doing in the saloon. Not that the kid would have told him. He'd been paid a dollar by the person who'd asked him to deliver the envelope to say nothing about its sender and to make sure Harry was unaware of its delivery. And the kid had performed this duty with ease, due chiefly to Harry's inebriated state.

It was only when Harry finally returned to the bank that he discovered the envelope. His hand shook as he opened it, certain that he knew the nature of its contents. And he was right. It was another note, a longer one this time.

Who killed Ali Toombs? Wes and Harry Hayes!
Who had Will Cord killed? Wes and Harry Hayes!
Who's for the hangman's rope? Wes and Harry Hayes!
The time is coming . . .

Harry staggered out the back door of the bank and threw up the contents of his stomach in the alleyway.

★ ★ ★

Cole was playing solitaire at a table in Roxy's Palace when Lew Rosen approached him.

'Now there's a game I play myself,' Lew said, easing himself into a chair opposite Cole. 'Find it kinda relaxin', don't you?'

Cole looked across at the newspaper proprietor. 'Some,' he said. 'Helps me to think, too.'

Lew nodded. 'Me too. Got anythin' special to ponder on?'

'Nothin' special.'

'Plannin' to stay in town long?' Lew asked.

Cole smiled. 'Seems I've been asked that a mite too often since I arrived. Not very welcomin', wouldn't you say?'

Lew laughed and took a cheroot from the case in his waistcoat pocket. He offered the case to Cole, who shook his head. Lew lit his cheroot, then said, 'Folks get curious in a town like this. Stranger comes in, shoots up the foreman of the Circle H, the biggest spread for miles, and which belongs to

60

the most powerful family hereabouts who don't tend to let things like that lie. Only to be expected that folk wonder who this fella is. 'Specially when he can draw as fast as you can, mister. Makes a person extra curious.'

''Specially a newspaperman,' Cole said. 'Right?'

Lew laughed again. 'Right. And old Esau at the livery tells me you asked about Joe Hayes. Like maybe you've been here before? Although I can't say I remember you, and I've been here near on thirty years now.'

'Funny,' Cole said. ''Cause I remember you. Then again, I was only a kid at the time, not the sort you'd notice.'

'*Now* you've got me *real* intrigued,' Lew said, puffing on his cheroot.

Cole flipped the cards over and stacked them in a neat pile. He pushed his chair back and stood up. 'Guess I'll keep you guessin' for the time bein', newspaperman,' he said.

And with that, he walked out of the saloon.

Lew watched him go. 'I'll get to the bottom of you yet, mister,' he muttered to himself.

★   ★   ★

Harry arrived back at his house, white-faced and **still** shaking from the shock of finding the note in his pocket. His daughter, Bella, saw him from the window as he half-fell out of the buggy. She watched with a mixture of disgust and pity as he staggered up the path.

Moments later, she confronted him in the hallway. She said nothing, but the look she gave him spoke volumes.

Harry stared back at her. 'Yeah, yeah, I know!' he growled. 'Had a few drinks. Don't look at me like that!'

Bella sighed. 'Oh, Pa!' she said. 'You've been on the wagon for months, what's started you drinkin' again?'

'Ain't none o' your business!' he shouted. 'Quit botherin' me!' He weaved his way towards the stairs muttering, 'Lew Rosen . . . filthy notes . . .'

'Pa?' Bella said. 'What — ?'

'Gonna have a sleep,' he said, pulling off his coat and dropping it on the floor behind him, and tossing his hat towards a hat stand in the corner of the hall. It fell short by a yard, landing on the floor.

Bella watched him climb unsteadily towards his bedroom, then she picked up his hat and hung it on the hatstand. Next she collected his coat from the floor and was about to hang it beside the hat when something fell from one of the pockets. It was an envelope.

Bella hesitated only a moment before opening the envelope and withdrawing the note from inside it. As she read the words on the sheet of paper, her eyes narrowed and a frown creased her forehead. What did it mean? Who was Ali Toombs? More importantly, could this be the cause of her pa starting to drink again? And if so, why?

★　★　★

When he left Roxy's Palace to head back to his office, an idea popped into Lew Rosen's head and he changed direction. Moments later, he was entering the sheriff's office. He met with Bud Randall, who was on his way out.

'Warren in there, Bud?' Lew asked.

The young deputy nodded. 'Yeah, he's in there. In a kinda strange mood, if you ask me.'

'What d'you mean?'

Bud frowned. 'Looks worried about somethin'. Got somethin' on his mind. But whatever it is, he ain't keen to share it with me. Maybe he'll tell you, Lew.'

'Maybe,' Lew said.

He watched the young man cross the street, then turned and went into the sheriff's office. Warren Speer was sitting behind his desk, staring at a law dodger in front of him. As he became aware of Lew's entrance, he flipped the paper over, face down on the desk. But not before Lew had caught a glimpse of the image on the front.

'Howdy, Warren,' Lew said. 'I need a

mite of information, and I reckon you can help me. Fact, I'm sure of it.' He looked meaningfully at the law dodger.

After a moment, Warren sighed and turned the law dodger face up. 'Guess there's no point in tryin' to hide this from you, Lew,' he said. 'You'd only start ferretin' around askin' awkward questions, so I'll show you. But it ain't for puttin' in the *Gazette*. Not for the moment, anyhow.'

He pushed the sheet of paper across the desk. Lew turned it round and stared at the now familiar face.

'So that's who he is,' he said. 'Ex-member of the Brennan gang, Wanted for murder, it says here, Warren. You gonna arrest him?'

Warren shook his head. 'Not just yet.'

Lew smiled. 'Now why's that, I wonder?' He was silent for a moment, then went on, 'Let me guess. That father-in-law of yours has told you to lay off for a while, just until he can be sure what Sanderson — or Chance, as his name seems to be — is plannin' to do here in Consolation. Am I right?'

Warren made no reply, just stared at the newspaper editor.

'Yeah, I guess I'm right,' Lew said, chuckling. 'Consolation's latest visitor has got Wes worried. Now that's real interestin', ain't it?'

'Yeah, but like I said,' Warren told him, 'this ain't for puttin' in that newspaper of yours. Maybe later, but not yet. All right?'

Lew sniffed. 'Well, I guess so. Although it goes against the grain to be witholdin' information from the public.' He took a last look at the law dodger, then pushed it back towards Warren. 'One of these days, Warren, you're gonna have to stand up to that father-in-law of yours. I just hope I'm still around to see it.'

After Lew left the office, Warren screwed up the law dodger and threw it across the room, cursing loudly. Wes had walked to the bank directly after leaving the sheriff's office, arriving just fifteen minutes after his brother had left the Horseshoe.

'Is my brother in?' he asked Ettings, the clerk.

Ettings was an old man with a grey beard that reached down to his cravat. He was sitting on a high stool behind a roll-top desk, surrounded by cabinets and files. A big box safe stood in the corner.

'I think your brother's gone home, Mr Hayes,' he said. 'He — er — wasn't feelin' well.'

'You mean he was drunk,' Wes said.

Ettings shrugged. 'Think I heard him leave by the back door 'bout five minutes ago.'

Wes swore softly and walked out of the building and across the street. He gathered up his horse which he'd left tethered to the hitching rail outside Roxy's Palace, then rode to the edge of town where Harry's impressive house stood. Joe Hayes had had it built when Harry had married Ellen Blaine, a girl from out East. She'd died fourteen years ago giving birth to a daughter, Bella, who now acted as housekeeper for Harry.

And now Harry was planning on marrying another woman from the East. A rich widow-woman who, from what Harry had told Wes about her, was a cut above the Hayes family, socially. Somebody who wouldn't understand the ways of the West and some of the things folk had to do to stay ahead of the game. And somebody who would drop Harry like a hot coal if she ever found out about his part in the Ali Toombs business.

So whoever was digging up all this stuff from the past, sending anonymous notes, had to be stopped. And it was no good leaving it to a booze-sodden Harry to take care of it.

'Hello, Uncle Wes,' Bella said, as Wes entered by the front door of Harry's house without knocking.

She was a plain girl, with cropped hair and thick eyeglasses. Her shirtwaist seemed to be straining to hold her plump figure inside it. An apron was strung round her middle. But she was capable and quick-witted, and Wes knew that she was pestering her father to send her East to one of the better schools, then on to college. But Harry liked having her around and was stalling.

'Where is he?' Wes asked.

'Sleepin' off his drunk,' Bella told him. Her disapproving tone was clear.

'So he's started drinkin' again,' Wes said. 'For Cris'sakes, that's all I need!'

'Just the last coupla days,' Bella said. 'He'd been on the wagon for months afore that. Don't know what's got into him, unless it were the note.'

'Note?' Wes's ears pricked up. 'What note?'

Bella took an envelope from the pocket of her apron and handed it to Wes. 'It fell out of Pa's pocket. Who's Ali Toombs?' she asked.

Wes didn't answer. As he read the note, anger welled up inside him.

'What's it mean, Uncle Wes?' the girl asked.

'Nothin',' Wes replied. 'Just some twisted joke.'

'Pa was mutterin' something about 'Lew Rosen and his filthy notes' when he came in,' Bella said. 'Is that who the joker is, Lew Rosen?'

'Maybe,' Wes said. He pushed the note into his pocket. 'When he finally wakes up, tell your pa I'll deal with this.'

Wes's first instinct was to charge down to the newspaper office and confront Lew Rosen with the note. Ask him what in hell he was playin' at. But caution stayed his hand and, instead, he went back to the Circle H. He needed to think on this, especially now that he knew Cole Chance was the stranger in town.

But something was to happen the next day that would send him charging into town as soon as he found out about it. Which was when Harry Hayes arrived red-faced and breathless with his copy of that Friday's *Gazette*.

5

Lew had barely arrived back after breakfasting at Nettie's eating-house when Wes Hayes burst into his office.

'What'n hell is this about?' Wes screamed at him, slamming Harry's copy of the *Gazette* on Lew's desk.

'Mornin', Wes,' Lew said, calmly. 'I was expectin' you.'

'Bet your dam life you were! And your life ain't worth a plugged nickel right now, Rosen.' Wes spat on the floor. 'Explain it — now!'

Lew glanced down at the 'Announcements' section of the newspaper, and the boxed announcement in heavy black type in the centre of the page.

Remember Ali Toombs?
She died an ugly death.

**Her killers were never caught and hanged
But now their time has come.**

'Don't exactly rhyme, does it?' Lew said. 'Makes a point, though.'

'Never mind that. Who placed it?' Wes demanded.

'Anonymous,' Lew said. 'Got back to my office yesterday aft'noon and found the sheet of paper with the words on it on my desk, together with twenty cents. That's the cost of a bold-type announcement, so I felt obliged to put it in the paper.'

Wes's eyes narrowed. 'I don't believe you. *You* wrote it and put it in the paper, admit it.' He pulled out the anonymous note that had been planted on Harry and slammed it down on Lew's desk. 'Same as you wrote this, and the other note.'

Lew picked up the sheet of paper and read the words twice, his head buzzing with thoughts. 'Interestin',' he said eventually. 'But nothin' to do with me,

Wes. Even so, seems like somebody's tuggin' your tail.' He smiled. 'Any truth in the — uh — accusation?'

Wes stared at the other man. Was Lew Rosen telling the truth? Did he really know nothing about the notes or the newspaper announcement? If so, then who . . . ?'

'No truth at all,' Wes said.

'Guess you ain't got around to readin' my editorial yet, Wes,' Lew said, a sly smile twitching at the corners of his mouth.

Wes stared at Lew a moment longer, then turned over the pages of the *Gazette* until he found the editorial. A minute later, he screwed the newspaper into a ball and hurled it across the room.

When he spoke, his voice was soft but deadly. 'That'll be the last editorial you'll ever write, Rosen,' he said.

Lew watched him leave, then went through to his living-room at the back of the office. He took a bottle and a glass from a cupboard and poured himself a large whiskey. His hand was shaking. He'd be lying to himself if he didn't admit to feeling like a man under sentence, but he was mighty curious about the anonymous note-writer and the person who'd left the announcement for the newspaper. One and the same? Lew reckoned so.

But who?

★   ★   ★

Wes was in no real mood for his usual games with Maggie Brown that morning, but something — habit maybe — took him across to the saloon and up to her room.

She was waiting for him, a half-open wrap over her naked body. For once it did nothing to arouse him, especially when he noticed a copy of the *Gazette* thrown carelessly on the floor by the bed. It was open at the page of the announcement. Wes wondered how many more *Gazettes* would be lying open at that particular page in houses and businesses across the town. Some people had long memories, people who would remember Ali Toombs. Others would be asking the question.

It was as though she'd read his thoughts.

'Who was Ali Toombs, Wes?' Maggie asked.

Wes turned away. 'How do I know?' he said.

'But you saw this in the paper about — '

'Yeah, yeah, I saw it!' Wes snapped. 'It don't mean nothin' to me.'

After a moment, she slipped off her wrap and climbed into bed, propping herself against the pillows. She waited, but he seemed in no hurry to join her.

'What d'you know about this guy Chance — er, Sanderson?' he asked.

He was staring out of the window and didn't notice her look of surprise at the question.

'Nothin',' she said.

He turned and looked at her. 'He was quick enough to come to your aid when

Jud Grey got a bit free and easy with you.'

'Didn't ask him to,' Maggie said. 'He just did.'

'Yeah, well, I don't take kindly to folks messin' with my men. Remember that next time.'

'Sure, Wes,' she said.

He began to pace the room. 'I'm thinkin' he's been in Consolation before. There were some homesteaders by the name of Chance hereabouts, twenty years or so ago. And that's his real name, so I'm told. A gunslinger.'

'And you think he's come back for a reason, Wes?' Maggie said.

Wes took a handkerchief from his pocket and wiped the beads of sweat from his forehead. 'How should I know?'

He stopped and looked at her, the bed covers around her middle, her breasts exposed. The sight of this still did nothing to stir his manhood and he gave an agitated wave of his hand.

'I'm goin',' he said, suddenly. 'Got

things to arrange.'

'OK, Wes,' she said. 'Same time tomorrow?'

'Maybe,' he said.

He had made a decision. At least one thorn in his side was going to be squashed.

★ ★ ★

Cole had been looking out of his hotel bedroom window when he saw Wes come into town and march directly into the *Gazette* office. Having seen a copy of the newspaper earlier whilst eating his breakfast in the hotel dining room, Cole had had a pretty good idea why Wes was in such an all-fired hurry to get to Lew Rosen. And it had presented him with an opportunity to go out to the Circle H and have a long-overdue chat with Joe Hayes without Wes's interference.

Now, as Cole topped the crest of a hill and looked down into the valley, he gazed at just part of the vast spread of the Circle H, and the sprawling stone-built ranch house beyond.

It took him a further twenty minutes' riding to reach the house. Two men were in the corral, and a third was coming from the bunkhouse as Cole drew his horse to a halt alongside the veranda. He recognized none of them, and they cast indifferent glances in his direction.

It would have been different if Jud Grey or Jim Ellis had seen him, he reflected. As it was, he made his way unhindered to the massive doors fronting the building.

Someone had seen him coming, because they opened before he'd had a chance to knock. A stout woman in a flowered pinafore stood framed in the doorway, a broom in one hand. Some sort of housekeeper, Cole guessed.

'Yessir?' she said.

'Come to see Joe Hayes,' Cole told her.

'He expectin' you?' she asked.

Cole smiled. 'Can't be sure about that. Maybe he's been expectin' me for the past twenty years, or somebody like me.'

She looked confused. 'Best step inside, an' I'll go see if'n he wants to talk to you. He ain't well, y' know.'

'I heard,' Cole said.

'What name?'

'Sand — ' Cole stopped, thought again. 'Chance,' he said. 'Cole Chance.'

She moved back so that he could step into the vast, oak-panelled hall. A massive sweeping staircase confronted him. An old long-case clock stood underneath it. Oak doors led into rooms right and left, and there was a passageway ahead.

'Wait here,' she told him.

She went away, leaving Cole with his thoughts. Last time he'd seen Joe Hayes it had been with his father. Evan Chance had taken his kid with him to the much more modest ranch house that Joe Hayes had occupied then. Why had his father taken him? Cole reckoned it had been in the hope of extracting a mite of sympathy for Evan's cause — getting a fair price for all that was left of the Chance homestead and land after the raging fire that had almost taken their lives.

Evan Chance had cursed Joe Hayes as he had tried in vain to put out the fire in the darkness of that terrible night, but when daylight had come he had known that there would never be any proof of who had started the fire. Sure, *he* knew that it had been Circle H men in the pay of Joe Hayes, but how to prove it? Hayes was a powerful man, protected by the local law that he'd bought and paid for and hiding behind a reputation as a so-called town benefactor, whereas in truth, folks were too afraid of him to argue with anything he wanted to do in or around Consolation.

No, the only thing to be done was to cut your losses and move on. Which meant Evan going begging to Hayes to try and obtain a fair price for all that was left after the fire. No crop, no paddock, no farmhouse, just the scorched land.

Fair price? What a hope! Hayes had

bought him out for a pittance. The bastard had —

Cole's thoughts were interrupted by the return of the housekeeper.

'Mister Hayes'll see you in Mr Wes's study,' she informed him. 'Follow me.'

She led him along the passageway to a room at the back of the house. The door was open and she left him to enter alone. Joe Hayes was sitting behind his son's desk, a mere shadow of the man Cole remembered.

'Well, Cole, you sure have grown a bit since you and your pa and ma lived around here,' Joe said, breathing heavily. 'You were a scrawny little varmint then.'

Cole stared at him, sickened by the old man's shrunken body, the skeletal skull, the wisps of grey beard.

Joe made a wheezing noise which Cole identified after a moment as being a laugh. 'Shocked, ain't you?' the old man said after a moment. 'Yeah, well, a dyin' man ain't a pretty sight. An' I'm havin' a partic'ly bad day today. So state your business and . . . ' He was

81

unable to finish the sentence.

'I was curious,' Cole said. 'Wanted to see again the man who killed — yeah, *killed* — my ma and pa.'

'Now hold on — ' Joe began.

'Oh, sure, you didn't put a bullet in them,' Cole said. 'Might have been better if you had. As it was, you burned them outa their home and forced them to move on. My pa died less than a year later. Just bone weary, the doc said he was. Used up by the effort of tryin' to start again. Ma died six months later — of a broken heart and a broken body, the doc said.'

Joe Hayes stared back at him. 'The fire . . . it wasn't meant to — '

'To what?' Cole growled. 'Burn the farmhouse? No, Pa reckoned it wasn't, at that. Just the crop, that's what he said you'd planned to destroy. Guess you didn't figure on the wind that night. Strong enough to pick up the fire and set the house ablaze. My ma, pa and me barely escaped with our lives.'

'I'm sorry, son,' Joe breathed, his

voice barely audible.

'No, you ain't,' Cole said. 'You'd do it all over again. Fact, from what I hear, your sons are followin' in your footsteps, burnin' folks' crops, foreclosin' on their mortgages. Still land-grabbin'. Ain't you got enough, for Chris'sake?'

The two men looked at each other silently, hate burning in Cole's eyes, defeat written across the old man's face.

'I came here plannin' to put a bullet between your eyes,' Cole said at last. 'But y' know what? I ain't goin' to do it. I reckon it'd be too kind. You're headin' towards a painful death, old man. A slow, painful death, and that's fine by me.' A savage smile curled the corners of his mouth. 'But maybe I ain't finished with your sons, not now I know they're no better'n you.'

And a feeling of satisfaction came over Cole as he saw the fear in the old man's eyes.

''Bye, old man,' he said. 'I hope you rot in Hell!'

And he turned and walked from the room.

★ ★ ★

After Cole had gone, Joe Hayes slumped forward on his son's desk. The shooting pain in his gut seemed to be cutting him in half and his head throbbed with a hammer-like pounding.

He gasped and wheezed, and it was a full minute before his breathing returned to something like normal. Then he sat back in the swivel chair and wiped a dribble of saliva from his lips.

What he needed was a drink. Didn't Wes keep a bottle of whiskey in his desk? Joe seemed to remember seeing his son taking a nip now and then.

He opened the drawer at his side.

No bottle. Instead there was a sheet of paper, half-crumpled, but the words on it plain enough to read. And, as Joe read them, a name leapt out at him, startling enough to reawaken the gut-wrenching pain in his stomach again.

Ali Toombs.

He'd never expected to hear or see that name again. That old business was dead and buried — or should have been. Hadn't he fixed everything years ago? What was the name of the kid he'd had framed? Cord, that was it. Will Cord. Well, he was dead, so it wasn't him raising ghosts. So who was it? And why hadn't Wes said anything about the note?

'Keepin' it from me,' he muttered to himself. 'Didn't want me gettin' upset. Darn fool!'

So what was Wes doing about it? Not letting it lie, that's for sure. Then Joe remembered Harry's visit the other day, and the haunted look on his older son's face. Was this what it had been about? Had *Harry* been the one who'd received the note, then brought it to Wes? If so, the sender had got it right, Joe thought. Harry was the weakest of his sons, the most likely to panic. Most likely to take to the bottle again and let loose with his tongue.

Joe began to think about the person who was stirring up this hornets' nest. His first thought was the man who had just left him. Had he been around at the time Ali Toombs had died? Could have been; Joe couldn't remember. But he would have been just a kid. Still, his pa could have said something . . .

Maybe I ain't finished with your sons, not now I know they're no better'n you.

Was this what Cole had meant? That he planned a campaign — a drip, drip of subtle threats — before going in for the kill? Or maybe Cole didn't plan to kill them *by his own hand*. Maybe he wanted to get them — Harry in particular — to condemn themselves, simply by scaring them into saying something incriminating. Not something that was likely to work with Wes.

But Harry?

Joe remembered how, at the time, Harry had gone to pieces and had needed to be sent East to stay with relatives to keep his mouth shut. Joe hadn't let him come back for a full two years, and by then Harry had found himself a wife.

By that time, talk of both Ali Toombs and Will Cord had died down, and the Hicksons had been dead for several months. Another 'unfortunate' fire had consumed their run-down farmhouse, with them inside it. No loose ends, the way Joe liked things.

At least, that's what he'd thought. But now a 'loose end' seemed to have surfaced, and become a threat.

Cole Chance?

Maybe, maybe not, but Joe Hayes wasn't a gambling man. If there was a potential risk to the safety or reputation of his sons, then it had to be dealt with.

A feeling of immense weariness and despair swept over him, but he came to a decision. It was time Jud Grey was given the opportunity to get his revenge.

6

Lew was devouring roast mutton and potatoes at Nettie's eating-house, washed down with mugs of strong coffee. Nettie sat across the table, watching him. He was early for lunch and her regular customers had yet to arrive.

'So who exactly was Ali Toombs?' she asked him.

It was the question a lot of Consolation townsfolk had been asking that morning, and getting answers from old-timers and long-term residents of the town.

Lew swallowed the last mouthful of mutton and gulped a swig of coffee before replying. 'Ali and her parents lived in town back in the 'sixties. Her pa was killed in the last year of the war, but her ma was an educated woman and taught school in the town. There was no schoolhouse, just an old barn.

But the handful of kids in the town at that time went regular like, up until the time Molly Toombs died of the fever.

'Ali was left an orphan at ten years old, and the only folks willin' to take her in were the Hicksons. They had a run-down farm and no kids of their own, so they saw Ali as useful. Treated her like a damn slave, if'n you ask me. Barely fed and clothed her. Fact, when she died, the Hicksons didn't spend much time mournin' her death, only regrettin' the fact that she was no longer available to do all the dirty jobs on the farm.'

'But Ali was killed?' Nettie said.

Lew nodded. 'When she was fifteen.' He took a swig of coffee, seeming unwilling to continue with the story.

'Well, go on,' Nettie said. 'How'd she die?'

'Choked to death,' Lew said, after a moment. 'Seems someone had been . . . takin' their pleasure of her, if you get my meanin', and things had got out of hand.'

Nettie looked shocked. 'Dear God,'

she said. 'Who?'

'Well, that's just it,' Lew said. 'Luther Hickson blamed a young man called Will Cord.'

'But you don't reckon he was right?'

'Reckon somebody put the idea in his head,' Lew said. 'Luther was a lazy, ignorant sonofabitch, and easily persuaded.'

'So who do you blame?' Nettie asked.

'The Hayes boys, Wes and Harry,' Lew answered with conviction. 'Like I said, a coupla hell-raisers they were at that time. Had any damn female who took their fancy, and Ali was a pretty little thing, in spite of the rags the Hicksons dressed her in.'

'What happened to Will Cord?'

'Shot in the chest while walkin' home from the Horseshoe. S'posed to have been Luther who shot him, but I ain't convinced of that. Oh, sure, Luther took the credit for it, but he was nearly loco anyway. Could be persuaded to think anythin' if he was paid enough money.'

'Was there any proof that this Will Cord killed Ali?'

'So-called proof, yeah. A tinplate locket belonging to Ali, and a letter purportedly from Ali sayin' that she was carryin' Will's baby and that she was plannin' to announce this to everyone if'n he didn't marry her. Both found in Will's pocket. Planted there, if'n you ask me. Oh, sure, Will had been a bit of a hell-raiser at one time, but he'd got himself a nice girl — Jane Duggan, daughter of the local preacher. Been goin' with her a year or more. Gonna marry her, he told me just a few weeks afore he was killed. No, he never touched Ali Toombs, I'd stake my life on it. It was the Hayes brothers, and it was old Joe Hayes who covered their damned tracks and got the blame put on Will.'

Nettie absorbed all this, then said, 'So that's what that announcement in the *Gazette's* all about.'

'Seems like it,' Lew said. 'Got Wes Hayes rattled, that's for sure.' He smiled. 'And that ain't no bad thing.'

'You be careful, Lew,' she said.

A few minutes later, Vince Chessman and Max Prentiss arrived. Following them in was a third man — Tom Bowman. The three of them sat at a nearby table, nodding to Lew.

Tom Bowman owned one of the few remaining homesteads not taken over by the Hayes brothers. But he was in trouble, as he explained to Lew. A month earlier, his corn crop had been burned — almost certainly not by accident. Now Harry Hayes was calling in Tom's bank loan, and Tom had no money to pay it. He'd been relying on money from his crop to clear the loan, but now it looked as if he was going to be another victim of the Hayes brothers' land-grabbing tactics.

'How much is it you need, Tom?' Lew said.

'Three thousand dollars,' Tom said. 'Might as well be a million, 'cause there ain't no way I can find it.' His eyes were tearing up. 'Had me that place more'n thirty years.'

'It's a darn shame,' Vince said. 'And here's me 'bout to lose my store.' He slammed a fist down on the table, sending cutlery crashing to the floor. 'We gotta do somethin', Lew. Those editorials in your paper ain't worth a spit if'n they don't change nothin'.'

Lew was forced to agree. 'Yeah.' He was thinking about the note Wes had shown him and the anonymous announcement in the *Gazette*. 'Sometimes words just ain't enough.'

'So what're we gonna do?' Vince said.

'What *can* we do?' Tom said, miserably. 'They've got you and me by the short hairs, Vince. Gonna take over your business and my farm in a matter of weeks unless we can come up with somethin'.'

'Or somebody else can,' Lew said softly.

'Eh?' Tom said. 'What d'you mean, Lew?'

Lew told them about the anonymous note.

'So somebody's tuggin' the Hayes

boys' tails,' Max said. 'Wonder who it is?'

'Know what I'm askin' myself?' Nettie said. She had brought a pot of coffee over to the table and was pouring the steaming liquid into the three men's mugs.

'What?' Max said.

'I'm askin' why now, after all these years? Why not before? What's happened to trigger it off now?'

'The last straw that broke somebody's back,' Lew put in. 'Somebody like Vince or Tom, about to see their livelihood disappear 'cause of the Hayes family. Somebody who's been in Consolation long enough to remember Ali Toombs and what happened to her. Somebody who didn't believe Joe Hayes's version of events at the time.'

'Somebody like you, then, Lew,' Nettie said.

Lew shook his head. ''T'weren't me.'

'Nor me,' Tom said.

'Me neither,' Vince said, 'although I wish I'd thought of it. Anythin' to get those bastards riled.'

'Can't see how it's gonna do you any good though, Vince,' Max said. 'Harry Hayes is still gonna foreclose on you.'

''Course it could be somebody new to the town,' Nettie said. 'Well, not *new*, 'xactly, but somebody who's been holdin' a grudge against the Hayes family for years and has come back to settle an old score.'

Lew was nodding. 'Yeah, now that's an idea, Nettie. Somebody like the stranger in town.'

'The Sanderson fella, y'mean?' Vince said.

''Cept his name ain't Sanderson: it's Chance. Cole Chance,' Lew told them. 'I had a word with Warren Speer and finally got it outa him. Cole Chance was a one-time member of the old Brennan gang.'

'Who're the Brennan gang?' Nettie asked.

'*Were* the Brennan gang,' Max said. 'Used to rob banks and trains. That's right, ain't it, Lew?'

Lew nodded. 'Finally disbanded after Rufus Brennan and his brother Cormac were killed in a raid. The two or three remainin' members of the gang split up and went their separate ways. Cole Chance was one of them. Warren's got an old law dodger with Cole Chance's name and picture on it.'

'So why ain't he doin' somethin' about it?' Tom asked.

Lew smiled. 'That's the interestin' thing. Wes Hayes told him to hold off for the time bein'. Now why would Wes do that, I ask myself?'

''Cause he suspects Chance is the note-sender?' Vince suggested.

'Right,' Lew said. 'And 'cause he's afraid of what 'xactly Chance knows about the Ali Toombs business. What he knows and what he might be able to prove.'

The three other men thought on this for some moments, then Vince said, 'Seems to me this Chance fella needs to watch his back.'

'There's somethin' else,' Lew said.

'Somethin' you and Max and Nettie won't know, but Tom might remember.'

'What's that?' Tom asked.

'Remember a man called Evan Chance? He used to have a homestead near — '

'Hell, yes!' Tom broke in. 'Course I do! Got burned out — not just his crop, but his cabin, too. Lucky not to be burned alive, from what I remember.'

'And he had a kid, didn't he?' Lew said.

'Yeah . . . but I can't remember his name,' Tom said.

'Me neither,' Lew said. 'Nor his wife's. But the kid coulda been called Cole, and — '

'And this fella Chance could be the kid growed up,' Max said. 'That what you're sayin', Lew?'

'That's what I'm sayin',' Lew agreed.

'And that would sure give him a powerful reason for hatin' the Hayes family,' Tom said.

'But again, why *now*?' Nettie wanted to know. 'Why not years ago?'

'He was too busy robbin' banks and trains,' Max said. 'But the Brennan gang broke up some years ago, so why's Chance waited until now? Unless he's been operatin' as a gunman on his own.'

'From what I hear about the skirmish in Roxy's Palace with Jud Grey, he sure ain't lost his touch with a gun,' Vince said. 'Faster'n anybody round here, that's for sure.'

'So maybe somethin' will turn up to save your two hides,' Lew told Vince and Tom. 'Maybe Cole Chance is your knight in shinin' armour, come to rescue you.'

Tom and Vince looked at one another and saw the flicker of hope in each other's eyes.

'I sure hope you're right,' Tom said to Lew. He looked at the clock over the door to Nettie's kitchen. 'I gotta see Harry Hayes at the bank this afternoon. Says he wants to talk to me about my loan. In other words, he's gonna start squeezin' me.'

'Best of luck,' Vince said.

7

Joe Hayes was sitting on the veranda outside the ranch house when Wes arrived back at the Circle H. Wes passed his horse to one of the ranch hands to take care of and walked towards his father. He immediately saw something was wrong by the expression on the old man's face.

'What is it, Pa?' he said. Then he saw the sheet of paper in his father's hand. 'Wh-where d'you find that?'

'Where you left it, Wes,' Joe rasped. He took a couple of laboured breaths, then went on. 'In your desk. Why didn't you tell me about it?'

Wes pulled up a chair and sat down by his father. 'Didn't want to worry you, Pa. It's nothin' I can't handle.'

'Oh, yeah?' Joe said. 'Now let me guess — Harry got the note, right? And Harry panicked and came runnin' to you.'

'Well, yeah . . . '

'And if I know Harry he's tried to drown the whole business in booze,' Joe gasped. 'Probably drunk as a skunk and shootin' his mouth off.'

'Sorta,' Wes admitted. 'Well, drunk, anyways. Bella's takin' care of him. He's sleepin' it off right now.'

Wes thought for a moment, then decided to go on.

'There's more,' he said. 'There was some damn-fool announcement in the *Gazette* today. Mentioned Ali Toombs. Said somethin' about her killers never bein' caught.'

Joe gave him a sharp look. 'And they weren't, were they, Wes?'

Wes coloured up but didn't answer.

'So who put the piece in the paper?' Joe asked, his breathing getting more and more laboured. 'Lew Rosen?'

'That's who I thought it was at first,' Wes said. 'Now I ain't so sure. There's this fella in town, Cole Chance, who — '

'He paid me a call,' Joe said.

Wes's eyes widened with shock. 'What!'

With an effort that almost over-whelmed him, Joe slowly managed to tell his son about Cole's visit. Wes listened with barely controlled patience as his father gasped out the words, then he stood up.

'I gotta do somethin' about Mr Chance,' he said.

'Already done it,' Joe said. 'Jud's gonna . . . take care of him.'

'Jud?' Wes gave a short barking laugh. 'Jud's already tried his hand at that. Nearly got himself killed.'

'It'll be different this time,' Joe said. 'He'll have surprise on his side.'

Wes looked less than convinced, but decided to say nothing. There was somebody else who needed attending to, and he would need a couple of his other gunslingers for that. Best to say nothing to his father about it though. The old man already looked to be at death's door.

★　★　★

Harry was conscious of Bella's disapproving stare as he climbed on to the buggy and drove himself towards the centre of town and the bank. His head hurt like hell and his tongue felt as if he had a mouthful of sand. Bella had made him eat something before he'd left, but already the food was threatening to quit his stomach.

Ettings watched him enter the bank with barely concealed contempt, but said nothing. Cy Carter reminded Harry that Tom Bowman was due to see him, and nodded to a chair by the door where Tom was waiting.

'Come into my office, Tom,' Harry said.

The other man followed him.

'Bring me some coffee, Cy,' Harry said, as he closed his office door.

'You don't look well,' Tom said, as he sat in the chair opposite Harry. 'Somethin' botherin' you?'

There was a half-smile that Harry didn't fail to notice. Well, he'd soon wipe that off the smug bastard's face, he thought. He waited until Cy had brought his coffee and left.

'Your loan, Tom,' he said. 'That's what's botherin' me. What're you doin' about it?'

'Ain't nothin' I can do, Harry, not since my crop got *accidentally* burned.'

'Accidents happen,' Harry said. 'Ain't nothin' I can do about that. It don't change anythin' as far as the loan's concerned.'

''Cept I was relyin' on that crop to pay all my bills, not just the bank loan,' Tom said. 'Now there ain't no money in the pot, other than a few dollars. Just about enough to put food on my table.'

Harry took a mouthful of coffee, wincing as he almost scalded his tongue. His head was pounding and he felt sick. 'Well, that's tough, Tom, but it don't solve my problem. Time's runnin' out on your loan. Got yourself just another week to sort somethin' out, is that clear?'

'A week?' Tom said. 'Oh, well. I guess a lot can happen in a week.'

Harry looked up sharply — then

wished he hadn't. He closed his eyes briefly, against the pain in his head. Then he said, 'What's that s'posed to mean?'

'Don't mean nothin' really,' Tom said. ''Ceptin' maybe a few skeletons can come outa cupboards and give people more important things to think about than loans.'

'What're you sayin'?' Harry snapped.

'Just talkin',' Tom said. 'Well, I gotta go, if'n that's all you gotta say to me.'

Harry watched as the other man stood up. Was there some sort of threat implied in those words about skeletons and cupboards? A thought pushed its way through the fog in his brain. Wait a doggone minute! Was Tom Bowman the person writing those notes and putting announcements in the *Gazette*?

'It's you, ain't it?' he said.

Tom was at the office door, and he turned round. 'Me, what?'

'You who sent them notes,' Harry said.

'Notes?' Tom said. 'What notes is

that, Harry?' The half-smile had returned to Tom's face as he went out and closed the door behind him.

★ ★ ★

It was early evening when Cole made his way to Roxy's Palace. He'd spent the last couple of hours debating whether or not to stay in Consolation, now that he'd seen Joe Hayes and had decided to let nature take its course. This Ali Toombs business was none of his affair, so what was keeping him here?

Maggie Brown?

What was it about her? For some reason he was unable to define, Cole found himself feeling protective of her. But what was there to protect her from, apart from hotheads like Jud Grey? The answer escaped him.

As he walked from the hotel, some sixth sense told Cole that he was being watched, possibly even followed, but when he looked round he could see nobody.

The saloon was three-quarters empty,

just a handful of men playing poker at a table, and two others at the bar. Cole recognized none of them. Three flouncy saloon girls sat on the stairs displaying an inviting amount of flesh and under-wear.

One of them was Maggie Brown, and she got up and walked across to the bar as Cole asked the barkeep to give him a beer.

'Evenin',' she said.

'Evenin',' Cole replied. 'Buy you a drink?'

'Thanks,' Maggie said. She nodded to the barkeep who poured some dark liquid into a glass and pushed it across to her. 'Word has it your name ain't Sanderson after all.'

He smiled. 'But you knew that, Maggie.' He lowered his voice. 'Same as I know your name ain't Brown.'

She dropped her own voice to match his. 'I was aimin' to talk to you about that.'

'No need,' Cole told her. 'Ain't none of my business. Person can change their name if they choose to, and I dare say you have your reasons.'

Maggie nodded. 'I have.' She decided to be bold. 'What were yours? Tryin' to forget your past? Seems I was told you were hooked up with the Brennan brothers.'

'A person can't really forget their past, Maggie,' he said. 'They can try and put it behind them and move on.' He stared at the array of bottles behind the bar, but she could see his thoughts were elsewhere.

'Last I heard, you were married and had a kid,' she said. 'What happened to them?'

His face darkened and he took a drink of beer before answering. 'Fever got them,' he said.

'I'm sorry,' Maggie said after a moment.

They were both silent for some minutes, then Cole said, 'We had a farm. I tried workin' it a few more months after Louise and Dan died, but couldn't stand it. Sold out to a neighbour. Been movin' around ever since. Then I remembered somethin' that needed doin' here in Consolation. Louise managed to put it out of my mind durin' the time we were together.'

'Somethin' involvin' the Hayes family?' Maggie asked.

He looked at her. 'Maybe.' His curt tone did not invite an explanation.

'What happened after the Brennan Gang broke up? No more banks and trains?'

'No, I'd had a bellyful of all that,' he said. 'Had me some money, and I lived on it for a few months. Then I got a job on a farm, owned by a man called Mike Hudson, a widower. Louise was his only daughter.' He stared into space, a faraway look in his eyes. 'Most beautiful gal I'd ever seen. Knew I wanted her the minute I laid eyes on her. I'd taken the name of Sanderson by then, but I knew I had to come clean about my past with Mike.' He chuckled. 'Darn me if'n Mike hadn't already guessed who I was. Seems he'd seen my face on some law dodger even before he'd employed me. Reckoned on givin' me a second chance. Well, then I told Louise, only to discover she knew about me and the Brennans, too.'

'And she didn't *care?*' Maggie asked, surprised.

'Did at first, after her father had told her who I really was,' Cole said. 'By the time I came clean about everythin', she'd changed her mind about me. We were married a week or two later. Then when her pa died in a ridin' accident the following year, I took over runnin' the farm. By then, we had Dan.'

'She sounds like a good woman,' Maggie said.

'Yeah, the best,' he said. 'I guess she reckoned she could keep me on the straight and narrow. Could, too. Even now, when I get a hankerin' for the old days, I only got to think about Louise, and it's enough to stop me doin' anythin' about it.'

'But you came here to do somethin',' Maggie said.

He sighed and nodded. 'Guess I can tell you,' he said. 'Had a mind to put an end to Joe Hayes, 'til I saw him earlier today, that is. Now I figure I'll just let nature take its course. He ain't got more'n a few more months to live by my reckonin'.

'What did Joe Hayes do to you?' she asked.

'Killed my ma and pa, good as.' He told her his story. 'I was eleven years old when my ma died. Went to live in an orphanage. Ran away when I was fourteen. Bummed around, got into some wild company, finally met up with the Brennan brothers.'

'And started robbin' banks,' Maggie said.

'I only ever shot and killed one man,' Cole said. 'A bank guard. And only then because he was goin' to kill me. But I've always been fast with a gun. Used to practise as a kid.'

'As Jud Grey discovered,' Maggie said. 'And it's my bet he ain't forgiven you.'

They were silent for some minutes,

concentrating on their drinks. After a time, Maggie said, 'You want to come upstairs?'

He looked at her, and her meaning was clear. 'Know somethin'?' he said. 'I ain't been with a woman since Louise died. Ain't wanted to . . . until now.'

She put down her drink and took his arm. Without another word, she led him towards the stairs.

* * *

The stocky figure of Jud Grey was stretched out in the darkness, on a roof across the street from Roxy's Palace. The flat roof belonged to the barbershop, next door to the office of the *Gazette*. Jud could hear Lew Rosen moving around in the room at the back of the newspaper office, but he paid no heed.

At his side was a Winchester. There was going to be no fancy gunplay this time, his injured hand didn't permit it. Just a straight shot. Then it would be goodbye Mr Cole Sanderson, or whatever your name was.

Jud had expected to have to wait until Cole exited from the saloon, so he was surprised, after the lamp in Maggie's room was lit, to see the man he was going to kill follow her in. He smiled.

'Well, well,' he muttered to himself. 'Ain't that a pretty sight. Don't reckon Wes'll be too pleased to hear about you takin' the gunslinger to your bed, Maggie. Then again, maybe I'll just save you the trouble of beddin' him.'

He picked up the Winchester and took aim at the lighted window. Maggie's back was to the window. Cole had moved out of the line of vision. Then, as Maggie stooped to step out of her chemise, he came into sight.

Jud lined up and fired — and the bedroom window disintegrated. He'd aimed to take Cole through the head, but missed. Cole dived to the floor, dragging Maggie down with him. Jud heard her scream clear across the street.

He cursed and began to move quickly to the tree at the back of the building, which he'd used to climb up on to the roof. He scrambled down and ran along the alleyway at the back.

But Jud knew he couldn't return to the Circle H until he'd done what he'd come to do — kill Cole. Joe's instructions had been clear.

'I want him dead,' Joe had told Jud. 'Don't come back until you can tell me that he is.'

He kept running, staying in the darkened alleyways at the backs of the church and schoolhouse.

*　*　*

Deputy Bud Randall heard the shot and the crash of glass. He'd been sitting in Warren's chair reading a penny dreadful, his feet on Warren's desk. The sheriff had left for home an hour earlier.

'Sounded like a rifle shot,' Bud muttered to himself.

He dropped his book on the desk and made for the door, putting a hand on his holstered .45. Outside, a few people had ventured out into the street. One of them, Lew Rosen, was pointing to the rooftop above the barbershop.

'Shot came from up there, Bud,' he said, as the young deputy reached him.

'Where'd it go?' Bud wanted to know.

Lew pointed across to the bedroom window above the saloon. 'Maggie Brown's room.'

'Who'n hell would want to shoot Maggie?' Bud said.

Lew shook his head. 'Tweren't Maggie who was the target.'

'Who then?' Bud asked.

Lew nodded towards the boardwalk outside the saloon where Cole Sanderson — or Cole Chance as more and more people were beginning to know him — was standing. He was scanning the rooftops opposite.

Bud walked across and confronted him. 'Somebody takin' potshots at you, Mr Chance?' he said.

'Seems like it,' Cole said.

'Now who'd want to do that?'

'Could make a guess,' Cole said.

'So make one,' Bud said.

'Jud Grey?'

Bud chewed his lower lip, thoughts swirling around in his head. Jud Grey worked for Wes Hayes, and Wes Hayes was Warren's father-in-law. Didn't pay to upset the town's most powerful citizen, and Wes might very well get upset if his foreman ended up in one of the cells at the back of the sheriff's office. And when Wes Hayes got upset, it was often his son-in-law who bore the brunt of his anger.

'Ain't got no proof of that,' Bud told Cole.

'Nope,' Cole agreed. 'Just a mighty strong suspicion. But don't worry, Deputy, I can take care of myself.'

'How's Maggie?' Lew Rosen asked him, having come across to join the discussion.

'A bit shaken, but OK,' Cole told him.

A smile twitched at the corners of Lew's mouth. 'Nice girl, Maggie. Very . . . accommodatin'.'

Cole raised one eyebrow but made no reply. Instead, he began to walk along the street, staying in the shadows, away from the streetlights.

★　★　★

Jud Grey watched his quarry walk away from Lew Rosen and the deputy sheriff. Impossible to make a shot from the alleyway where Jud was hiding, the angle was all wrong. He had to hope that Chance was heading back to the hotel. Once inside, Jud would have no trouble entering the back of the building without being seen and sneaking up to Chance's room.

And he was in luck! Chance was indeed making his way to the hotel. Jud watched him go inside, and was almost tempted to take a shot when the other man was silhouetted in the lighted doorway. But again there was no guarantee he'd hit his target.

He could wait.

First thing was to check and see which room Chance was occupying. Just a matter of seeing which lamp was lit. Likely the clerk had given Chance a front room, and — yes! there it was. The room over the hotel entrance was suddenly illuminated. But Chance was being careful. No shadow passed across the window before a blind was drawn down.

Didn't matter. Jud had no plans for a second distance shot. Next time it would be up close when his target was sleeping. And with a blade.

Meantime, he'd get himself a drink.

8

Harry Hayes was in the Horseshoe saloon at the time Jud had taken his potshot at Cole Chance. He was only half-aware of the sound and, although others in the saloon had ventured outside to see who was shooting at who, Harry had remained at his table, the bottle of gut-rot whiskey comfortingly clutched in one hand, his glass in the other.

He was thinking about Tom Bowman and the farmer's remarks about skeletons in cupboards. Tom hadn't actually mentioned the name Ali Toombs, but Harry was becoming more and more convinced that it was her death Tom had been referring to.

Not that there weren't a few other skeletons in the Hayes's cupboards, but it seemed to Harry to be too much of a coincidence for the remark not to be linked to the anonymous notes and the announcement in the *Gazette* to which Bella had drawn his attention earlier, frightening the hell out of him. Then he'd immediately thought of Lew Rosen as being the person responsible. After all, it was his damned newspaper. But now Harry wasn't so sure. More and more he was beginning to favour Tom Bowman as the guilty party.

Tom knew that the burning of his crops was no accident, and that it was almost certainly down to some of Wes's men. And Tom had been around at the time of Ali Toombs's death, and probably suspected Harry and Wes of the killing.

Harry shivered and poured himself another whiskey. Images of Ali's ravaged body kept surfacing in his head. What had he and Wes been thinking dragging her off into the forest of pine trees? Taking their pleasure of her. Of course, if she hadn't struggled . . .

Harry screwed his eyes shut and tried to banish the images from his mind.

Instead, he thought about Coleen and their forthcoming wedding. Except there probably wouldn't be any wedding if Coleen ever learned the truth about Ali Toombs. She was a church-going, somewhat strait-laced lady with strong moral values. If she thought her husband-to-be had once taken part in the rape and murder of a young girl, she would head back East as fast as the first stage could carry her, thanking God for a lucky escape.

No, this mess had to be sorted out before Coleen arrived. There could be no more anonymous notes or announce-ments in the *Gazette*. Whoever was doing this had to be stopped.

Harry didn't see Jud Grey enter the saloon and make his way to the bar. But he heard the other man's voice.

'Whiskey,' Jud told the barkeep.

Harry opened his eyes. What was Jud Grey doing in town? Why wasn't he at the Circle H? Maybe he was about to find out, as the other man had seen him and was coming across, clutching a glass.

'Evenin', Mr Hayes,' Jud said.

Harry was aware of the critical eye that was passed over him by the Circle H foreman. OK, so he was drunk; so what?

'What you doin' in town, Jud?' Harry's words were slurred and he blinked against the light as he looked up at Jud.

'Bit of business for your father, Mr Hayes,' Jud said. He winked. 'Best not to talk about it, though.'

Both men drank in silence for some minutes. Then Harry said, 'You hear about the crop fire at Tom Bowman's place?'

Jud's eyes narrowed. 'Yeah, I heard.'

'He's plenty mad, I reckon,' Harry said.

'He is?' Jud said. 'Well, I guess it's to be 'xpected.'

'Makin' veiled threats to me when I saw him in the bank earlier,' Harry told him.

'Threats about what?' Jud asked.

Harry looked at him for a moment,

deliberating. Then he said, 'Never you mind.'

Jud drank his whiskey in one gulp. 'Want me to take care of him, Mr Hayes?'

'Nope,' Harry said. He spat on the floor. 'C'n take care of him myself.'

A dubious expression passed across Jud's face, but he chose not to argue. 'OK, Mr Hayes,' he said. He looked at the clock over the bar, which said that it was eleven o'clock. 'Gettin' kinda late, ain't it? Didn't you oughta be makin' your way home?'

Harry scowled. 'Go when I'm ready, won't I?' He slopped more whiskey into his glass.

Jud stood up. 'Well, I got that bit o' business to attend to, so I'll be leavin' you.'

Harry watched Jud leave, a fuzzy mist seeming to have settled in front of his eyes. But at least the pain in his gut had been deadened by the alcohol, and a soothing warmth had spread over him.

Can take care of him myself, he had

told Jud, referring to Tom Bowman. Could he though? Harry took another gulp of whiskey. Damned right he could! Do it first thing in the morning. Take himself out to Tom's place and put an end to those damned notes. Put an end to Tom Bowman! Show Wes *he* could handle things on his own. Dammit, *he* had been the strong one in the old days! Well, maybe it was time he was the strong one again.

A stab of uncertainty came into his thoughts, but he pushed it away. He'd make it look like a robbery by some passing stranger. Take a few things from the farmhouse — money if he could find any.

Of course, it meant writing off that loan, didn't it? No, wait, he could take and sell the farmhouse, which had been the surety against the loan.

Harry smiled. Everything was going to come out OK.

★ ★ ★

As Jud came out of the Horseshoe, he checked the room over the hotel entrance and grunted with satisfaction when he saw that the window was in darkness. Crossing the street quickly, he made his way down the side of the hotel building to the small door at the back. It was unlocked, as he had expected. In Consolation where criminal activity was rare, few businesses locked their doors. Other than the bank, only Buck Tarmy, who kept the gun and ammunition store, bothered to secure his premises at night.

Jud eased the door open and moved silently along the passage to the back stairs. Climbing them in the darkness — hands outstretched, fingers probing — was dangerous, but he made it to a landing where a single lamp was lit for the benefit of hotel guests who came in late.

Jud counted the doors along the landing and worked out that the door to the room above the hotel entrance was the middle one. He crept towards it, wincing as a floorboard creaked, tried the door handle — yes! — and smiled as he found it unlocked. He placed his Winchester on the floor and, removing his knife from its leather sheath on his belt with his good hand, he eased the door open slowly. Cold sweat prickled on the back of his neck. The room was in darkness, but there was enough light from the moon coming through the flimsy blind over the window for Jud to see the humped shape in the bed.

Holding his breath, he crept towards it, paused momentarily, then slammed the knife downwards — *and knew immediately that it wasn't a body under the bed covers*, just rolled blankets and a pillow. He'd been fooled!

Confirmation of this fact came seconds later.

'Wrong room, Jud,' said a voice behind him.

Jud whirled to see Cole Chance standing in the open doorway, the light from the landing behind him glinting on the barrel of the .45 that he was holding.

'How in hell — ?' Jud began.

'I'm in the room next door,' Cole said. 'Checked with the clerk to make sure this room was unoccupied before I played my little game with the lamp and the blind. Figured you'd be watchin' the hotel, and that you'd make your move sometime durin' the night. Seems I was right.'

Jud swore vehemently, but made no move.

'What're you gonna do?' he asked.

'I'm gonna turn you in to the sheriff, Jud,' Cole said.

'He ain't there.'

'No, but his deputy is. I took the trouble to check after I played my little game. Left the hotel by the back door, of course. Returned the same way. Yep, young Bud Randall should be waitin' for us right now.' Cole waved the .45. 'So, let's be goin'. There's a cell waitin' for you.'

Jud gave a short laugh. 'Randall can

126

lock me up, but he sure as hell can't keep me there, not when Wes hears about it. He'll have me outa there in no time.'

'Maybe, maybe not. I reckon Wes Hayes has got other things on his mind right now. Come on, move! And leave that knife behind.'

Jud dropped the knife on the bed and moved towards the doors. At that moment, there were footsteps in the passage, then a voice called, 'What's goin' on here?'

It was the desk clerk, and the momentary distraction gave Jud the opportunity he needed. As Cole glanced behind him into the passage, Jud threw himself at the other man and sent him flying backwards through the doorway. The report from the .45 as Cole fired it echoed through the building as both men crashed to the floor. The bullet embedded itself in the ceiling before the Colt spun from Cole's hand.

Seeing the two men wrestling with one another, the startled clerk gave a yell and ran back to the stairs.

Although hampered by his injured hand, Jud was a strong man and quickly pinned Cole to the threadbare carpet covering the floorboards. He hit Cole with a crushing blow which Cole took high on one cheekbone. In reply, Cole jabbed the knuckles of his right hand into Jud's Adam's apple, cutting off Jud's supply of air.

Gasping for breath, Jud rolled off Cole. As he rolled, he drew his own .45, took aim and fired. The slug caught Cole on his left shoulder. At the same time, Cole's boot lashed out and caught Jud on the kneecap. Jud screamed with pain, but was already levelling his pistol for another try at killing Cole.

Cole snatched his gun from the floor where it had fallen, squeezing the trigger in the same movement. The bullet caught Jud in the centre of his forehead, smashing him back against the door frame, where he slumped in a heap.

'Guess you won't be needin' that cell

after all, Jud,' Cole muttered, conscious of the blood seeping through the shoulder of his own shirt.

Moments later, the clerk emerged from the top of the stairway. His face was ashen and he stared at Cole with a mixture of awe and fear. Another bedroom door opened and a fat man in a striped nightshirt took in the scene before hastily retreating back into his room.

'Get Deputy Randall,' Cole told the clerk.

'Y-yessir.'

'And the town undertaker,' Cole added. 'And maybe the doc for me.'

9

Wes waited until after midnight for Jud's return and the news that Cole Chance was no longer a threat. When Jud still hadn't come back, he began to fear the worst.

Confirmation of his fears came in the small hours when a group of his men who had gone to Consolation for a bout of drinking and womanizing returned with the news that Jud was dead. They had been leaving Roxy's Palace at the same moment that Jud's body was being removed from the hotel. One of the Circle H men had confronted Deputy Bud Randall and had got the story of Jud's failed attempt to kill Cole Chance. The motive for the attempt was being attributed by Randall to the earlier gunplay between Jud and Cole over Maggie Brown at Roxy's Palace.

Wes slept badly the rest of that night.

The following morning, he gave his father the bad news. The old man's sunken cheeks seemed to withdraw even further as he sank deeper into his chair.

'Jud was one of our best men, Pa,' Wes said. 'A good foreman.'

Joe Hayes shook his head. 'He was a gunman,' he croaked. 'But clearly no match for Chance.'

'Seems I'll have to do the job myself,' Wes said.

His father gave him a scornful look. 'You're no gunman, Wes. That's why you buy the services of others.'

Wes shrugged. 'OK, I'll send some of them.'

'He'll be on his guard,' Joe said. 'Won't be easy.' He took some gasping breaths, then went on, 'Maybe you should let the law take care of him. After all, he's a wanted man.'

Wes nodded. 'Maybe you're right. I'll go talk to Warren.' He hesitated. 'S'posin' Chance knows somethin' about Ali Toombs? Somethin' he can prove?'

'Like what?' Joe said. 'He was just a

kid at the time.'

'So you don't think he's behind these notes Harry's been gettin'?'

'No, I don't. My bet's Lew Rosen. We ain't his favourite people, never have been. And now you're puttin' pressure on some of his friends, like Vince Chessman and Tom Bowman. He ain't gonna like that. Then there's them editorials he's been writin' in the *Gazette*, attackin' you. Another one this week, ain't there?'

'Yeah.' Wes smiled. 'But I've got a plan to put a stop to them. Just got to go over it with a couple of the boys.'

Joe looked at him and sighed. 'I don't want to hear about it. I'm too old and too tired for all this.'

'OK, Pa.'

'And Harry? What about him and his drinkin' and his loose tongue?'

'Leave Harry to me, Pa,' Wes said.

★ ★ ★

Joe Hayes went out on to the veranda and sat in the cane rocking chair.

Damn it to hell! How had it come to this?

If he was honest with himself, he knew the answer. Fact was, he should've kept a tighter control over those two boys for the past thirty years. Should've put a stop to some of their more fool-hardy schemes, especially during the last four or five years when they'd thought they could get away with anything, as long as they bribed or threatened people. Hadn't caught on to the fact that some folks — like Lew Rosen, for instance — *couldn't* be bribed or pressurized.

After their mother died, when they were still little kids, Joe had left them pretty much to their own devices. He'd been too busy building up the Circle H and earning the confidence of local people. And, he had to admit, some-times *buying* the prestige and influence that he had eventually acquired locally. So maybe Wes and Harry had simply followed his example, but taken it to extremes. Difference was, he could read people. Knew when to push forward and when to back off, whereas Wes and Harry had just steamed ahead like a locomotive without brakes.

His biggest mistake with the pair of them had been the Ali Toombs episode. A warning sign if ever there was one about how far down the road to disaster his two hell-raising sons were heading. Oh, sure, he'd acted fast. Cleared up the mess. But it had meant doing something which had haunted him ever since — saving the hides of his two wayward sons by sacrificing the life of an innocent man.

Joe put his head in his hands. 'Gettin' old,' he muttered to himself. 'Can't deal with this kinda thing any more.'

* * *

At that moment, Harry Hayes was aboard his buggy heading towards Tom Bowman's farm. He'd slept the night in a room at the Horseshoe, the barkeep there having decided Harry was too drunk to get himself home. It wasn't the first time he'd had to give a drunken Harry Hayes overnight accommodation.

Harry's head pulsated and thumped with every bump and rut on the trail. He felt sick in the stomach and the mid-morning light, storm-laden though it was, was burning his eyes. Even so, his resolve to deal with Tom Bowman hadn't weakened since his decision the night before. Those notes had to stop; Harry couldn't take any more of them, and the threats they implied. Whatever Tom Bowman reckoned he knew about the Ali Toombs business was going to die with him.

Black clouds, both real and metaphorical, hung over him as he rattled along in the buggy. The first drops of rain sent up puffs of dust from the parched earth. There was a jagged streak of lightning, followed moments later by a clap of thunder which rolled and echoed through the purple-black sky, and resounded around him.

The rain came in a sudden downpour, sweeping across the landscape and soaking Harry's business suit in minutes. He wore his black Stetson pulled low over his unshaven face, but no slicker. The hoofs of his horse splashed through deep puddles, throwing up water on to the buggy. Harry ignored it. Barely noticed the thunder and lightning. Cared nothing about his drenched and ruined suit.

Ten minutes later, he was within sight of the blackened remains of Tom Bowman's burned-out crops. The rain had eased slightly and the rumbles of thunder had drifted away into the distance.

Harry pushed a hand under the buggy seat and withdrew the Winchester which he'd taken without asking from under the bar at the Horseshoe. He'd already checked that it was loaded.

'Time's runnin' out for you, Tom Bowman,' he said aloud. 'You and your damned notes.'

★　★　★

Lily Bowman saw the buggy coming as she looked out the window of her kitchen. She had been washing dishes but paused to stare at the approaching vehicle. It was some minutes more before she could identify the driver.

'Harry Hayes is comin'!' she called to her husband, who was in the parlour, going through the bills that seemed never to cease coming from local traders.

'Comin' *here*?' He hurried through to the kitchen and looked out of the window. 'What'n hell does he want?'

'No doubt we'll find out in a few minutes,' Lily said.

They watched as the buggy drew closer.

'Dammit, he's got a rifle!' Tom said. 'I ain't never known Harry Hayes to carry any kinda weapon since the days when he was a hell-raisin' kid.'

With that, he gathered up his own Winchester from a shelf behind the door.

'Don't do anythin' stupid, Tom,' his wife advised.

'Ain't aimin' to,' he said. 'But I aim

to be ready in case Hayes does.'

Minutes later, the buggy came to a stop outside the farmhouse door. They watched as Harry climbed down from it, the rifle under one arm.

Tom opened the door and stood on the step outside, his own Winchester tucked under his arm.

'Mornin', Harry,' he said. 'Not like you to come visitin'. In a storm, too.' He nodded towards the rifle under Harry's arm. 'And I ain't seen you carrying a gun since we were both kids. What's on your mind?'

'Scarifyin' notes, that's what's on my mind,' Harry snarled. 'Notes which you ain't got the guts to put your name to. Announcements in the *Gazette*. Tauntin' remarks about skeletons in cupboards, that's what's on my mind. I'm aimin' to put a stop to them.'

'You've got it all wrong, Harry. I ain't sent any notes. Didn't put any announcement in the paper, neither. You've got the wrong man.'

'Liar!' Harry shouted. 'What's all this

'truth about Ali Toombs' you're gonna tell? Ain't nothin' *to* tell. Will Cord killed Ali Toombs, remember? Luther Hickson shot him. It's all history.'

'Maybe it is, maybe it ain't. Some folks have other ideas about it.'

'And you? You got any ideas?' Harry's eyes blazed, and he lifted the Winchester to point at Tom. 'Speak, damn you!'

'Maybe I have,' Tom said calmly. 'Never believed Will Cord was the culprit. He was all set to marry the preacher's daughter, Jane Duggan. Pretty little thing, she was. Why would he force himself on Ali Toombs? Nope, reckon he was innocent. Reckon some other varmint — or maybe *two* varmints — set on her.'

Tom saw beads of sweat begin to form on Harry's forehead. The Winchester suddenly looked sticky and uncomfortable in the other man's hands.

'They say she was a real mess,' Tom went on. 'Legs bleedin', clothes torn, face cut and bruised. What kinda animals do that to a young girl, Harry? The drunken, hell-raisin' sort, I reckon, don't you?'

A faraway look came into Harry's eyes as if old, terrifying images were forming in his head. The Winchester began to shake in his hands.

Tom sensed the change in Harry's demeanour and pressed on. 'Then there was Will Cord, cut down in a dark alleyway at night.'

'Shut up!' Harry shouted. He pressed an arm to his chest, as if to ease some sharp pain. He looked to Tom as though he badly needed a shot of whiskey.

'A note was planted on Will's body to make it look like he'd made Ali pregnant,' Tom went on imperturbably. 'Old Doc Partridge, who was the medic in Consolation at that time, told Lew Rosen confidential-like that Ali wasn't pregnant at all. Lew, bein' Lew, couldn't keep it to himself. Told it to old Esau Parker at the livery, and Esau told me.'

'It's all lies!' Harry screamed. 'Shut

your filthy mouth, Bowman!'

''Course the sheriff at that time was in the pay of your Pa, Harry. Nothin' anybody told him was goin' to change anythin'.'

Tom kept a careful eye on Harry's rifle as he talked, his finger curled around the trigger of his own Winchester in readiness. He knew he'd been taunting the other man, but somehow he hadn't been able to stop himself. All these years he'd suspected the Hayes brothers of being the cause of Ali Toombs's death, but like others he'd been unable to prove it. He'd kept his suspicions to himself, voicing them only in the company of his friend Lew Rosen. For years the truth had been suppressed, for fear of a backlash from Joe Hayes. Too many people in Consolation were 'owned' in some way or another by the Hayes family, either through bank mortgages and loans, or because of things Joe Hayes knew about them that they wouldn't want made public.

But now it seemed somebody was about to blow the Ali Toombs business wide open again with anonymous notes and announcements in the local newspaper.

'Feelin' scared, Harry?' Tom said. 'Get the feelin' things are unravellin' around you? Maybe it's time the Hayes family — '

It was as far as Tom got before Harry's Winchester cracked and the shot whined past Tom's left ear and embedded itself in the doorframe behind him. Before he could get off a second shot, Tom had dropped his own rifle and thrown himself off the step, knocking Harry backwards on to the mud-slick ground.

The two men wrestled in the ooze and slime, but fat, soft, overweight Harry was no match for the leaner, fitter Tom Bowman. Tom was fast and well versed in the rough-and-tumble of a brawl. As a kid, he'd been in a scrap almost every day. Now, as the two men rolled around, kicking and punching,

Harry's ineffectual blows were countered by hard-hitting thumps that sent bright lights whirling behind his eyes and knocked the breath out of his body.

Sensing victory, Tom relaxed and pushed himself up on to his hands and knees. Harry lay unmoving beneath him, eyes shut, breath coming in painful gasps.

Tom grabbed Harry's Winchester as he stood up. With one swing, he smashed the rifle against the farmhouse steps and broke it. Then he threw it into the buggy.

He held out a hand. 'Get up, Harry. Take yourself home.'

Harry ignored the proffered hand. Slowly, painfully, he got to his feet. 'It ain't over, Bowman,' he said. 'For one thing, there's still your loan. I ain't aimin' to forget that.'

'Didn't think you would,' Tom said.

He watched as the manager of Consolation's only bank — suit ruined, face and hands bloody and covered in mud — pulled himself on to the buggy seat and drove away.

Tom's wife emerged from the house, her face pale, her hands screwing her apron into a ball in front of her.

Tom turned to her. 'Guess we're for it now, Lily.'

'Guess we are,' she said, her voice a frightened whisper.

★ ★ ★

A defeated, dejected Harry sat slumped in the buggy as he drove back to town. It had all gone wrong. He'd been humiliated. What was worse, he still hadn't solved the mystery of the anonymous notes. Something about Tom Bowman's unwavering stance and forceful denials had made him doubt his earlier conviction that Tom was the culprit.

Hell, he'd been a fool to go rushing out there! What the blazes was Wes going to say? Or his pa, when the old man came to hear about it, as he would? There would be the devil to pay, that was for sure.

He needed a drink, badly. First stop was going to the Horseshoe. He needed a shot of redeye before he could face the sneering look of Ettings. He would know nothing about his visit to Tom Bowman, of course, but just lately the senior clerk seemed to sense the downturn in Harry's fortunes.

A mile from Consolation, Harry felt a stabbing pain in the upper part of his body. It seemed to shoot down his left arm, and suddenly he was unable to breathe.

'Jesus!' he gasped, dropping the horse's reins and clutching his chest.

The horse and buggy kept moving, but Harry's eyes were screwed tight against the agonizing, vice-like grip of the pain. Moments later, blackness descended over him and he slumped further down in the seat of his buggy.

It was where two surprised citizens of Consolation found him when the horse, unerringly following the trail, finally trotted back into the town's main street.

Doc Tully was called, and within moments the white-haired medic had pronounced Harry dead.

10

Wes was with Maggie Brown when Roxy came knocking at the door of her room.

'Maggie?' Roxy called. 'Open up, I need to talk to Wes.'

Seconds later, Maggie opened the door. She was wearing a hurriedly thrown-on wrap, her face flushed from the exertions of a few moments earlier. Roxy's rotund figure pushed past her into the room. She was breathing heavily, having run up the stairs.

Wes was shoving his shirt-tail into his pants. 'What'n hell do you want, Roxy? Can't a man — ?'

'It's your brother, Wes,' Roxy cut in.

'Harry?' Alarm flooded through Wes like a tidal wave. 'What's he sayin'?'

'He ain't sayin' anythin' any more, Wes. He's dead.'

Wes looked stupefied. 'Dead? Who

— who killed him?'

'Nobody killed him,' Roxy told him. 'Although judgin' by his face he looks as though he's been in a fight. But Doc Tully reckons it was a heart attack that did for him. He says he's been warnin' Harry about his drinkin' and his excessive weight for some months now. T'aint no real surprise that his heart took him in the end.'

'Been in a fight?' Wes said. 'Who'n hell would Harry have been fightin' with?'

'His buggy came in from outside town,' Roxy said. 'And his suit was soaked and covered in mud. Reckon he was out there in that thunderstorm we had earlier.'

Wes's head was reeling. First Jud dead, now Harry. What was happening? And how, for Chris'sakes, was he going to break this latest news to his father? It could kill the old man. He finished dressing and strapped on his gunbelt. Without another word to either Roxy or Maggie, he stormed out of the room and down the stairs. After he'd gone, the two women looked at each other.

'There's gonna be hell for somebody to pay,' Roxy said. Then she left the room.

Maggie finished dressing and carefully brushed her hair. Her reflection in her dressing table mirror showed a satisfied smile on her face. Things were working out even better than she'd hoped.

* * *

Warren Speer came out of the Horseshoe at the same moment Wes exited Roxy's Palace. The two men caught each other's eye and headed towards one another. They met in the middle of the street.

'I hope you've got some answers about Harry's death,' Wes challenged the young sheriff.

Warren held up a hand. 'Now hold on, Wes. I've just been talkin' to Hal, the barkeep at the Horseshoe. Seems Harry spent the night there.'

'Why?' Wes wanted to know. 'Too drunk to make it home?'

'Somethin' like that.'

'So what happened to him this mornin'?'

'Hal reckons he went out to see Tom Bowman. Apparently he was mutterin' Bowman's name all through the cups of coffee Hal was feedin' him first thing to sober him up.'

'Why would he want to see Bowman?' Wes asked.

Warren shook his head. 'Beats me. But he took the Winchester Hal keeps behind the bar.'

'Harry was goin' to call in Bowman's bank loan next week, so I guess it could have somethin' to do with that. But why go all the way out to the Bowman farm? And why take the Winchester? Harry and guns parted company years ago.'

'Tom was in town yesterday,' Warren said.

'He was?' Wes said. 'Where'd you see him?'

'Came out of Nettie's and headed

across the street,' Warren said.

'So he could've been headin' for the bank.'

'Yeah, I guess he could at that.'

'Roxy says Harry looked as though he'd been in a fight,' Wes said. 'That right?'

Warren nodded. 'Looked like it. I planned to go out to Tom's place and ask a few questions.'

'When?'

'Right now.'

'I'll come with you,' Wes said.

Both men made a beeline for their horses.

* * *

Lew Rosen watched Warren and Wes ride out of town. He was seated at a table near the window of Nettie's eating-house, a pot of coffee in front of him.

Nettie came across and stood behind him. She watched the two riders over Lew's shoulder.

'Headin' for Tom Bowman's place, I

reckon,' Lew told her.

'You do?' Nettie said. She sat herself down in the vacant chair the other side of Lew's table. 'Why?'

'Just a hunch,' Lew replied. 'Tom had a meetin' with Harry Hayes at the bank yesterday. I saw Tom afterwards and, from what he told me, he had some fun tuggin' Harry's tail about those notes. 'Reckon he thinks I sent 'em' was Tom's remark. If'n that was the case, Harry could well have got himself riled up enough to pay Tom an unfriendly visit early this mornin'.'

'People are sayin' Harry looked pretty beat up,' Nettie said.

Lew nodded. 'He was. Been in a fight. And I reckon — '

He stopped as the door to the eating-house opened and Cole Chance came in. Cole nodded to Nettie and Lew, then sat at one of the empty tables, dropping his hat on the floor next to his chair. Part of a bandage showed under his shirt at his left shoulder.

Nettie made her way across, wiping her hands on her apron. 'What can I get you, Mr Sanderson?'

Cole smiled at her. 'It's 'Chance', Nettie. Most folk seem to know that now so there's no need for any more subterfuge. I'll take a pot of coffee and some of those fresh-baked rolls I can smell. And maybe a chunk of cheese.'

'Sure thing, Mr Chance,' Nettie said, and shuffled off into the kitchen.

'So Jud Grey's dead,' Lew said from across the room.

Cole looked at him for a moment, then said, 'That's right.'

'Hear you shot him.'

Cole smiled. 'Guess you hear most things that go on in this town, Mister newspaper editor. Did you hear the whole story?'

'Sorta pieced it together from what the clerk at the hotel told me. Heard Jud took a pot shot at you earlier in the evenin', too.'

'No way of provin' that,' Cole said. 'But I reckon it was him.'

'Seems a mite drastic as a means of revenge for some itty-bitty disagreement over Maggie Brown,' Lew opined. 'Think there might have been another motive behind the attacks?'

'Could've been.'

Nettie returned with a steaming pot of coffee and a plate of rolls, butter and cheese. She put them on Cole's table and hovered for a moment. Seeing that she'd somehow stalled the exchange between the two men, she discreetly returned to her kitchen.

'I've got a notion Jud was *instructed* to kill you,' Lew said, picking up the conversation where it had left off.

If the statement was intended to shock or surprise Cole, it failed. He spread butter on a roll, cut off a chunk of cheese and poured himself a cup of coffee. Only then did he say, 'You reckon?'

'Yeah,' Lew said. 'Tell me, you didn't by any chance leave twenty cents and a sheet of paper in my office the other day, did you? A sheet of paper with an announcement to be put in the newspaper?'

Cole smiled again. 'I think I know the announcement you're referrin' to. Interestin', I thought, but no it wasn't me who wrote and paid for it. You tellin' me you don't know who it was?'

Lew stared at him for some moments, then said, 'Well, I guess I am, if it really wasn't you who wrote it. I had it marked down to you, Mr Chance. That and the notes.'

'Notes?' Cole said.

'Yeah, notes. Somebody's been rufflin' the Hayes's feathers with some anony- mous notes.'

'Referrin' to the same subject as the newspaper announcement?'

'Yep.'

'And you reckon Wes Hayes thinks I'm responsible for them, and that he ordered Jud to — er — shorten my life?'

'Wes or Joe Hayes. Don't reckon it was Harry. Seems Harry might've had his own idea about who's sendin' them, albeit he got it wrong. Certainly ain't Tom Bowman sendin' them.'

Cole drained his coffee cup and poured himself some more. 'So who do you put your money on, Mister editor?'

'With you out of the picture? Can't begin to guess. Has to be somebody who was around here at the time Ali Toombs was killed, and who's got a grudge against the Hayes family. Don't make sense otherwise.'

'Guess you're right.'

The two men were silent for a time whilst Cole munched his way through his cheese and rolls, and Lew finished his pot of coffee.

Cole studied the other man. 'I was readin' your latest editorial in the *Gazette*. You sure don't aim to make yourself popular with Joe Hayes and his sons.'

'Ain't my job to be popular,' Lew said. 'My job is to ask questions and print the truth. And speakin' of questions, there's one I've been askin' myself.'

'What's that?'

'How come Warren Speer ain't arrested you? A one-time member of the Brennan Gang with a price on his head.'

'And what answer have you come up with?' Cole asked.

'Warren could be a good lawman, given half a chance.' Lew said. 'Trouble is, he's under his father-in-law's thumb. Gotta do what he's told. Like a lot of people in this town, he's owned by the Hayes family and, in his case, married into it. Left to himself, Warren would probably have arrested you by now. So the only reason I can come up with for his holdin' back is — Wes Hayes. For some reason Wes wants to keep you a free man.'

'Why? So he can have me killed by the likes of Jud Grey?' Cole said.

'Maybe. If you're dead, you can't talk. And I reckon Wes — or possibly even Joe Hayes — thinks you've got somethin' to say that they don't want people to hear.'

'Like?' Cole said.

'Like the truth about Ali Toombs's killin'.'

''Cept I'd left town before then. And anyway, I was just a kid.'

'Your pa could've told you somethin'.'

'Well, he didn't.'

'But Wes and his father don't know that.'

Cole shrugged. 'Guess I'll have to continue watchin' my back then, like people have been tellin' me.'

Lew smiled. 'Guess you will.'

'You too, Mister newspaperman,' Cole said.

11

Tom Bowman saw the two riders as he came out of his barn. They were coming fast towards his farm, like they had urgent matters to discuss. Tom felt a stirring of unease. What now?

The light was poor under the slate-grey sky, but he was soon able to identify them. And knew at once that their visit could only be bringing troublesome news. But about what? And why the *sheriff?*

Had to be to do with Harry Hayes. Maybe Harry had complained about getting beaten up and sent packing earlier. Wes wouldn't have taken too kindly to that. Tom was also pretty sure that Wes would have known nothing about Harry's visit until after the event. Was probably angry with Harry for coming out here shouting his mouth off.

Lily Bowman saw the riders as she swept the veranda at the front of the farmhouse. Like her husband, she also identified them at a distance, and came to the same conclusions as he had. That the visit had something to do with Harry's beating. A ripple of fear ran through her body. Everyone knew that when Wes Hayes was angry, he went half-loco and was liable to do anything.

By the time Wes and Warren reined their horses to a halt outside the barn, Tom had prepared himself for the torrent of words that spewed from Wes's angry mouth. But the wild look in Wes's eye and the Winchester he was carrying in his hand was a shock.

'Stay right where you are, Bowman!' Wes yelled. 'What did you do to my brother, you bastard!'

'Now hold on, Wes,' Tom began.

'Never mind 'hold on'!' Wes screamed. 'You beat him up!'

'It wasn't like that, Wes,' Tom said.

'What happened, Tom?' Warren asked. 'Harry's face was marked up pretty bad.'

Tom caught the past tense. ' 'Was'?' he said, fear suddenly invading his stomach like a viper's bite.

'He's dead, Tom,' Warren said.

'Yeah, and you as good as killed him!' Wes shouted, aiming the Winchester at Tom's chest.

Warren put out a warning hand. 'Now hold on a minute, Wes,' he said. 'Doc said Harry died of a heart attack.'

'Yeah, after the exertion of a fight with this bastard!'

'What was the fight about, Tom?' Warren asked.

Tom's heart was pounding but he tried to reply calmly. 'Harry had some crazy idea that I'd been sendin' unsigned notes and writin' that announcement in the *Gazette*, the one about Ali Toombs. He came out here totin' a rifle. Sent a bullet past my ear.' Tom nodded towards the farmhouse. 'It's bedded in my doorframe, if you want to take a look.'

'If he shot at you, then he had good reason,' Wes shouted. 'You had no call to beat him up.'

'I had to take the gun away from him,' Tom said. 'Else he would've killed me.'

'Tom!' Lily cried. 'Is everything all right?' She was hurrying towards her husband, carrying the Winchester that she'd collected from the house.

'It's OK, Lily,' Tom said. 'Just some misunderstandin'.'

'Ain't no misunderstandin' as far as I'm concerned,' Wes shrieked. 'You thrashed my brother and, as a result, he had a heart attack. That's as good as murder!' He was shaking with fury, his face crimson, his gun hand trembling. 'You're gonna hang, Bowman, and I'm gonna have the pleasure of stringin' you up!'

'Wait, Wes,' Warren said, naked fear evident in his voice. 'There's gonna be no hangin' until we get things clear.

'No hangin'?' screamed Wes. 'Then the bastard is gonna die now!'

And with that, he fired two wild shots, the first missing Tom by a foot or more, the second taking him in the chest and throwing him backwards into the doorway of the barn, where he lay, dead eyes staring at the sky.

Lily screamed, and without thinking raised the rifle and fired at Wes. The shot missed him, but it was sufficient to make him swing round and return fire. The slug hit her high on her left breast, hurling her to the ground. She didn't move.

★   ★   ★

'Jesus, Wes!' Warren cried. 'You've killed her! You've killed them both!'

Spittle was dribbling from Wes's mouth and his eyes blazed with a depraved satisfaction. 'They had it comin' !' he said with a quiet venom. Then he turned to Warren. 'And that's what you're gonna tell folks, Warren. You're gonna tell them Tom Bowman tried to kill me but accidentally shot and killed his wife. Then he shot himself.'

'For Chris'sakes, Wes!'

163

'*That's the story!*' Wes yelled. 'Got it? Accidental killin' and suicide.'

'I can't do it, Wes,' Warren began. 'You've just shot and killed two people. I can't — '

'You can and you will.' Wes looked coldly at the sheriff. 'You'll do as I tell you, Warren, same as you always do.'

For once, Warren was unable to keep the disgust out of his voice. 'One of these days, Wes, you'll push me too far. If it wasn't for Lucy, I'd get as far away from Consolation as I could get.'

'Yeah, but until then you'll do as you're told. We're goin' back to town, and you're goin' to see Zeke Laine about attendin' to the bodies.'

★　★　★

On the journey back to Consolation, Warren wrestled with his conscience. But, as always, hard-headed realism won out. Even if he told the truth about what happened at the Bowmans' farm, Wes Hayes would never see the inside of a prison cell or feel the touch of a hangman's noose. Old Joe Hayes would see to that. Dying he may be, but he still had some powerful friends in the territory. Friends who owed him favours from the past, or were still indebted to him financially.

Even so, the more he heard and saw, the more Warren was beginning to wonder if there wasn't some truth in the rumours that Wes and Harry had killed Ali Toombs, either accidentally, or on purpose, and that Joe Hayes had somehow managed to get the blame put on Will Cord.

But whoever was rattling these skeletons in the Hayes family's cupboard was now responsible for at least three more deaths, possibly four — Harry Hayes, Tom and Lily Bowman, and maybe Jud Grey if the unsigned notes and newspaper announcement were the motive behind Jud's attempts on Cole Chance's life. And at least three of those people had no connection at all with Ali Toombs, as far as Warren knew.

It was all getting out of hand. Maybe he'd talk to Lucy about moving on and starting afresh, somewhere a hundred miles from Consolation and the poisonous influence of her father and grandfather.

12

Word about Tom and Lily Bowman's death spread faster than a prairie fire. Most townsfolk seemed to swallow the story the sheriff put about, but a handful of people didn't believe a word of it.

One of them was Lew Rosen, and the newspaperman confronted Warren in the sheriff's office.

'Warren, you're feedin' folks a load of bullshit,' he said. 'You and I know there ain't a word of truth in the story you're handin' out.' Lew put up a warning hand as Warren tried to speak. 'No, don't try and convince me otherwise, 'cause I ain't a fool. Nor are a few other folk around here. Your reputation in this town's takin' a nosedive, and you should know this. It's time you stood up to those evil in-laws of yours. Time you made a stand.'

'I — I know what I saw,' Warren said, his voice shaking.

'Sure you do, and it ain't what you're tellin'. Zeke Laine says Tom Bowman was shot in the chest. Now nobody takes their own life by shootin' themselves in the chest.' Lew put two fingers — imitating a gun barrel — to his forehead and then under his chin. 'That's where they shoot themselves if they want to be sure of doin' the job properly.' He gave Warren a look of disgust. 'And Zeke says the shot that killed Tom was fired from at least six feet away. There were no powder burns on his chest, the way there would've been if the barrel had been against it when the gun was fired. Maybe I'll include those bits of information in the report I write up in the paper. Let folks come to their own conclusions about what really happened. Might even bring out a special edition of the paper.'

Alarm spread across the sheriff's features, but he clamped his lips together and said nothing.

'What's wrong, Warren?' Lew said. 'Cat got your tongue?'

With that, he turned and marched out of the office.

For a full five minutes after he'd gone, Warren sat at his desk, unable to move or think clearly. How had he let things get so out of hand? What in hell was he going to do? Lew Rosen wasn't going to let this matter rest, that was certain. And all hell was going to break loose if he really *did* print what he was threatening. Wes had been crazy. Killing Tom and Lily Bowman had been a step too far. Plain murder, no less.

The return of Bud Randall roused Warrren from his reveries.

The young deputy took one look at his boss and said, 'What's wrong, Warren? You sick?'

Warren avoided the question. 'Where've you been?' he said.

'No place special,' Bud replied. 'Just took a walk around town. Folks are busy speculatin' about what happened out at the Bowmans' farm. A few of them saw you and Wes Hayes ridin' out earlier. They say Wes looked murderous after what happened to his brother. Guessin' he must have threatened Tom Bowman somehow for Tom to take a potshot at him. How come Tom accidentally shot Lily? She standin' close to Wes Hayes?'

'Yeah,' Warren said after a moment. 'Yeah, that's how it was.' He stood up, pushing his chair back so violently that it crashed to the floor. Ignoring it, he walked past Bud and out of the door.

Bud stared after him, scratching his head.

'Somethin' ain't right,' he muttered to himself.

★   ★   ★

Warren tracked his father-in-law down in Roxy's Palace. Wes was sitting alone at a table in a corner, a whiskey bottle and a shot glass in front of him. The bottle was already three-quarters-empty and, judging by his father-in-law's high colour and the glazed look in his eyes, Warren guessed it had been full when Wes had started drinking.

Before Warren could cross the room to him, Roxy appeared and put a hand on his arm.

'What's wrong with Wes, Warren?' she said. 'I ain't ever seen him drink like that.'

'Shock, I guess,' Warren said. *Or guilt?* he thought.

'Yeah, I guess you're right. What with his brother dyin' like that. Then to see Tom Bowman kill himself after shootin' his wife, it's enough to drive anybody to the bottle.'

'Yeah,' Warren said, moving away from her.

He went to Wes's table and pulled up a chair.

'You OK, Wes?' he asked.

'Sure I am,' Wes answered. The words came out slurred.

'You told Joe about Harry yet?'

'Nope,' Wes said. 'Guess word will have got to him by now. Two of the

Circle H men were in town earlier, gettin' stores. News will have got back.'

The two men were silent for a moment, then Warren said, 'Lew Rosen paid me a visit.'

'What about Lew-bloody-Rosen?'

'He ain't convinced Tom Bowman shot himself.'

Wes gave a short barking laugh. 'So-bloody-what? So he ain't convinced. Ain't as though he can do anythin' about it.' He sloshed more whiskey into his shot glass, spilling as much on the table as went into the glass.

'I ain't so sure about that,' Warren said. 'Apparently Zeke Laine told him there were no powder burns on Tom's chest, so it was impossible that he could have shot himself. Reckons the shot came from at least six feet away.'

Wes downed the whiskey in one gulp and poured himself another. 'So?'

'So Lew's gonna mention that fact in the *Gazette*. Let people make up their own minds about what happened to

Tom. Says he might bring out a special edition of the paper. I'm worried, Wes.'

'Well don't be,' Wes told him. A smile spread slowly across his face. 'Lew Rosen ain't gonna be writin' anythin' in the *Gazette*. Not after tonight. Ain't gonna be no *Gazette* to write in!' This was followed by an insane burst of laughter.

'F'Chris'sakes, Lew!' Warren said, alarmed. 'What're you plannin' now? No more killin', you hear? I won't stand for it.'

'I won't stand for it!' Wes mimicked. He shoved a finger under Warren's nose. 'You'll stand for whatever I tell you to stand for, *you* hear? Just go home and stay there.'

★   ★   ★

Maggie watched Warren and Wes from a vantage point on the balcony above the saloon floor. She was dressed in her flouncy working outfit, but she was in no mood to entertain members of the opposite sex. In fact, she was feeling slightly sick. Roxy had told her of the events at Tom Bowman's farm. Maggie hadn't known either Tom and Lily Bowman, but she knew they'd been good people. Honest, hardworking, caring sort of folks. The kind of folks she'd have liked to have had as parents.

Maggie's mother had died giving birth to her. Maggie knew this, having been constantly reminded of it by her mother's two spinster aunts who had reluctantly taken on the responsibility of bringing Maggie up.

Familial love had been no part of the arrangement. Both the twin sisters had been in their fifties, had no experience of bringing up children, nor did they *like* children, and they made no secret of it. Assuming the role of surrogate parents had been considered by them to be no more and no less than a Christian duty, but not a welcome one.

Discipline had been their watchword, and the rules and regulations which they imposed on their young ward had been rigidly, not to say cruelly, enforced. Indeed, Maggie had been regularly beaten and locked in a darkened cupboard for the most trivial misdeeds.

At the age of seven she was sent away to a Chicago boarding-school, coming back to the great-aunts' house only for vacations. Then, at the age of fourteen whilst at home for the summer vacation, she had stolen fifteen dollars from a china coffee pot where her great aunts kept cash for emergencies, and had run away. With her, she had taken just a change of clothes and an old journal that she had found in her aunts' attic earlier that year. The journal, she had discovered, was a record kept by her mother, right up to within a few days of her death.

Maggie had never returned, and thought it highly likely that the two spinster ladies — who were by then nearly seventy — had made very little effort to find her. Probably thought themselves well rid of her.

Maggie had travelled west, hooking up with a wagon train leaving St Louis, after being taken in by a childless couple who had given up hope of ever having a youngster of their own. The wily fourteen-year-old had quickly recognized the couple's desperation as a means of getting a free ride and had rapidly ingratiated herself with them. On their part, the couple had instantly succumbed to Maggie's (albeit fraudulent) charms and had asked no questions about her background.

Ten days after leaving St Louis, the wagon master had also succumbed to Maggie's rather more ripening charms and had deflowered her for the princely sum of two dollars.

Fifty miles later and after lying about her age, Maggie had sneaked off from the wagon train to work in a saloon in some two-bit western town whose name now, five years later, she couldn't even remember.

It had been just the first of many saloons that had acquired Maggie's services over the next few years. Slowly, she had worked her way across country to end up where she had always intended — the Arizona town of Consolation.

The name of the town had been familiar to her for some years by that time; familiar because it had featured greatly in her mother's journal, which she had read from cover to cover.

As had the names of some of the people who were in Consolation when her mother had lived there, one of whom Maggie was staring at from her vantage point on the balcony of Roxy's Palace.

Wes Hayes.

Looking at him, she was sure of one thing: Tom Bowman hadn't killed himself, nor had he accidentally shot his wife. Both deaths, Maggie was certain, were down to the ruthless Wes Hayes. A revenge killing after the death of Harry Hayes, even though Tom Bowman had not actually killed Harry. Maggie had heard — via Roxy — that people were saying Harry Hayes had had a fight with Tom, and his heart attack was the result of that. And the reason for the fight? Something about anonymous notes, people said.

Which was why Maggie was feeling sick right now.

13

Cole found out about the Bowman killings when he overheard two men talking at the bar in the Horseshoe saloon. Cole had decided to give the Horseshoe his custom that evening rather than go to Roxy's. His reason was Maggie Brown.

She had been on his mind a lot lately and he needed to think about her without the distraction of her actual presence. In her he recognized a kindred spirit. Someone who had seen hard times, and whose character had been formed by similar trial and adversity in her years of growing up.

But something about her bothered him, something he couldn't pin down. And it wasn't just the fact that, underneath all that paint she applied to her face, he suspected there was a beautiful young woman. So what was it?

Something somebody had said? Something he'd overheard? Cole had become an habitual eavesdropper in the days when it had been important to keep one jump ahead of the law, and it was a habit hard to shake.

He couldn't remember the name of the town where he had first met Maggie. It had been one of those places he'd drifted through after leaving the Brennan gang and before meeting Louise. That he'd bedded Maggie he felt sure, although even the memory of that had coalesced with the memory of a dozen other soiled doves. But sometime during the past couple of days he'd caught some stray remark which had almost made a link with something he knew from, or had heard in, the past. A link his brain wanted to make with Maggie. Trouble was, he couldn't remember what it was.

He had been pondering this when he'd overheard the two men talking about the Bowman killings and had turned his attention to them. The name

Bowman had rung a bell. He remembered it had been the name of a couple who'd had the beginnings of a farm not far from his parents' homestead when he was a boy.

Now they were dead, and it seemed the two fellas at the bar were having trouble accepting the story that Tom Bowman had accidentally shot his wife and then killed himself.

'I don't believe it,' one was saying. He was a short, stocky man with a salt and pepper beard. 'Tom was always careful with guns. Never liked the things.'

'Even so, it could've happened if Lily had been wrestlin' with Wes Hayes and got in the way,' his friend countered. 'Seems Tom and Wes were arguin' over Harry Hayes's death, so Wes could've had a gun on Tom, and Lily could've been tryin' to get it off him. Could've happened that way, Ned.'

'If she *had've* been wrestlin' with him, Tom would never have taken a shot,' Ned said. 'Wouldn't have risked it.'

'So what're you sayin'? That Wes

Hayes killed 'em both?'

Ned looked round anxiously. 'Ain't sayin' nothin'. T'ain't healthy to speculate 'bout things like that in Consolation.'

'Guess you're right at that,' his friend agreed.

Cole finished his beer and walked back to the hotel. As he crossed the street, he noticed the glow of a lamp in the *Gazette* office, and he could see Lew Rosen hunched over a typewriter pecking away at the machine. Writing another inflammatory editorial for the paper? Cole wondered. He smiled. There was a man who wasn't intimidated by the Hayes family. Brave? Maybe. Some would say foolish.

★　★　★

It was after midnight when the two Circle H men rode into Consolation, the scuffing of their horses' hoofs, the creak of leather and the soft jangle of tack the only sounds in the street as the town slept. The two or three lamps still burning in buildings cast their light across the main street and spread the shadows of the two riders.

'You happy about this?' Chet Gilman asked his riding companion, in a low voice.

Jim Ellis hawked and spat on the ground. 'Sure I am. Wes is right. That blamed newspaper man is gettin' too uppity by half. Has to be stopped.'

Chet continued to look and feel uncomfortable. 'Then why don't Wes do his own dirty work? What d'you care about his damned editorials, or me for that matter?'

'Quit bellyachin',' Jim told him. 'It's what he pays us for, ain't it? Just make sure you've got the fuses lit and the dynamite ready to throw after I've busted the office window.'

'OK,' Chet said, after a moment. 'But I sure as hell don't like it.'

They rode on, two shadows moving through the moonlit street, while the unsuspecting citizens of Consolation dreamed their dreams.

Cole had been sleeping for less than an hour when he was woken by the noise of the explosion.

Dynamite!

His brain registered the word almost before his eyes were open. Immediately alert, he jumped out of bed and ran to the window.

Across the street, flames were coming from inside what remained of the *Gazette* office, which wasn't much. Sparks, flames and thick plumes of black smoke curled into the moonlit sky.

Cole pulled on his shirt, pants and boots. By the time he reached the street, others were emerging from buildings, some still in their night-clothes, and already a chain of men was forming to pass buckets of water to try and stem the course of the fire. There was little hope of saving the newspaper office, or Lew Rosen's quarters behind it, but there was a good chance the fire could be stopped from spreading to other buildings if the firefighters acted quickly.

'Where's Lew?' somebody shouted. 'Anybody seen him?'

'He was inside earlier,' came a reply. 'Saw him tappin' away on that type-writer machine of his.'

Cole joined the line of men passing buckets. The heat from the newspaper office singed his hair and eyebrows and his face was scarlet within minutes. Sweat poured down from his forehead, stinging his eyes.

There was the ominous groaning and cracking of burning wood before part of the roof caved in. Sparks flew into the night sky and the searing heat intensified, driving the firefighters back.

More men joined the chain, but it still took best part of an hour before the flames consuming the structure of the building began to subside, although debris from the explosion had ignited some of the heaps of paper and newsprint. These took more time to extinguish. But as for Lew's much-loved old printing machine, it soon became evident that it was nothing more than a twisted wreck of metal now.

When at last all that was left were hissing, sputtering blackened heaps of rubble, Doc Tully pushed his way to the front of the smoked-stained fire-fighters.

'I'm goin' in to look for Lew,' he said.

'I'll come with you,' Max Prentiss said.

The two men put scarves against their mouths and disappeared into the smoke that was still drifting out of the destroyed building.

'Took at least four or more sticks of dynamite to do this much damage,' said a voice from behind Cole.

He turned to see Deputy Bud Randall standing at his shoulder.

'Where's the sheriff?' Cole asked him.

'Home,' Bud said. 'Left the office early this afternoon. Not like him, matter of fact. Guess he wasn't feelin' well or somethin'.'

Or something, Cole thought. *Like he'd been expecting trouble and didn't want to be around when it happened.*

After a time, a shocked Max Prentiss emerged from the remains of the building and threw up at the side of the street. He was followed by an equally grim-looking Doc Tully.

'Did you find Lew?' Bud Randall asked the doctor.

Doc Tully nodded. 'What was left of him.'

'Jesus!' Bud said. 'As bad as that?'

As an answer, the doctor nodded in the direction of Max Prentiss.

'Jesus!' Bud said again.

'Best fetch your undertaker,' Cole told him.

'Yeah,' Bud said. 'But first I need to ask somethin'.' He turned to face the small crowd of people. 'Did anybody see who done this?'

There was silence for a moment or two, then a voice said. 'I saw two men ridin' out of town like the devil himself was after them.'

'Did you recognize them, Ed?' Bud asked.

The man called Ed hesitated. 'Reckon they could've been Jim Ellis and Chet Gilman,' he said eventually.

'From the Circle H?' Bud said.

Ed nodded. 'I reckon.' He looked uncomfortable.

'When was this? Before or after the explosion?'

'Just a few seconds before,' Ed replied.

'You mean, like they'd thrown the dynamite and then ridden off?'

'Yeah, 'xactly,' Ed said. 'See, I was havin' trouble sleepin', and I heard a crash like a window bein' broken. So I got up to look out of my window — my shop is a little way up the street from the *Gazette* office, as you know, and on the same side, so I can't see the newspaper office window from mine. But I reckoned that's where the crash came from. Anyway, it was then I saw the two men ridin' hell-for-leather outa town. Then seconds later came the explosion.'

'Sounds like they smashed the *Gazette* office window to make a hole for the dynamite to go through,' Bud said.

The crowd was silent, pondering on the enormity of the implications. Two Circle H men prime suspects for blowing up the newspaper office and killing Lew Rosen. One thing everybody knew but didn't say: Jim Ellis and Chet Gilman wouldn't have done it of their own volition. They would have been under orders — from Wes Hayes or his father.

'What're you gonna do about it, Deputy Randall?' Cole asked quietly. 'Can't let it lie.'

Bud had started to sweat, and it wasn't because of the heat from the ashes of the newspaper office. Cole could almost read the thoughts spinning in the young man's head. *Circle H employees, under instructions from the most powerful man in the town — in the whole territory, some said. The man who was Warren Speer's father-in-law.*

'It's cold-blooded murder,' somebody said at last.

It was enough to open the floodgates, and others took up the cry.

'Yeah, that's right!'

'Murder! Bloody murder!'

'The Hayes family have gone too far this time!'

'Gotta do somethin'!'

Heads had turned towards the young deputy, who was shifting from foot to foot and wringing his hands.

'I've gotta talk to Warren,' he said at last. 'He's sheriff in this town. Ain't my decision. First off, I'm gonna get Lew's body removed. Gonna fetch Zeke Laine.'

He elbowed his way through the assembly and headed towards the undertaker's parlour.

Gradually, the crowd began to disperse, heading back towards their homes and their beds. Not that most folk would sleep easy that night — or what was left of it. The fire at the newspaper office, the gruesome demise of the *Gazette's* editor, both coming so soon after the deaths of Harry Hayes, and Tom and Lily Bowman — it was the stuff of nightmares. Never in the history of Consolation had so many folk died in one twenty-four-hour period.

Cole was making his way back to the hotel when he noticed a figure huddled in her nightclothes and standing on the boardwalk outside Roxy's Palace.

Maggie Brown.

He hesitated, then changed direction and walked across to the saloon.

'You OK?' he asked her.

Her hands were thrust deep into the pockets of her wrap, and the face above her hunched shoulders was wide-eyed and white. She didn't seem to hear him, so Cole repeated his question.

After a moment, she seemed to realize he was there.

'What? Oh, yeah, I — I guess so.' Her voice was shaking.

'I guess Lew Rosen was a friend of yours,' Cole said.

She nodded. 'Yeah. Treated me like a lady.' She gave a grim chuckle. 'That's a joke, ain't it? Me, a lady! But that's how Lew treated me.'

'Probably recognized a certain quality in you that others don't notice,' Cole said. 'Who's really hidin' behind all that war-paint you put on your face, and the powder you put on your bosoms, Maggie? I get the feelin' there's more to you than meets the eye.'

She pulled her wrap tighter around her. 'Is it right some Circle H men did . . . that?' She pointed at the remains of the newspaper office.

'Seems likely,' Cole said.

'Why?'

'Can't be sure,' Cole said. 'But Mr Rosen seemed to go out of his way to ruffle the Hayes family's feathers in those editorials of his. Some of them must've stuck in Wes Hayes's craw.'

'Yeah, you're right.'

Maggie seemed somehow consoled

by Cole's reply, making him wonder about something.

'Were you thinkin' there might've been another reason?' he said. 'Like that announcement he printed in the paper about Ali Toombs? From what I hear, Wes Hayes was powerful angry at Lew for printin' that. Reckon he suspected Lew wrote it himself.' His eyes narrowed as he looked at her. ''Cept you and I know Lew didn't, don't we?'

That brought two spots of colour to her cheeks.

'Don't know what you're talkin' about,' she said, unconvincingly.

Cole smiled. 'Yes, you do, Maggie.'

'I — I need a drink,' she said, turning quickly and pushing through the batwings behind her.

After a moment, Cole followed her.

There were a handful of others in the saloon, drowning their sorrows, or taking an alcoholic palliative to calm their nerves after the shock of the night's events. Roxy, in her nightclothes like some of her customers, was behind the bar. She looked across to see Maggie come in and sit herself down at an empty table.

'You look as though you need a drink, Maggie,' she said, taking a glass and pouring a shot of whiskey into it. She took it across to the girl and put it in front of her.

'I'll take one, as well, Roxy,' Cole said, coming up behind the saloon owner and sitting down on the chair opposite Maggie.

Roxy looked at each of them, then went to get Cole's drink. She brought back a glass and a bottle. 'Help yourself,' she said to Cole. 'Reckon Maggie might need more than one. Looks as though she's had a fright. Guess we all have.'

Cole waited until Roxy had returned to her place behind the bar, then said, 'You paid to put that announcement in the *Gazette*, didn't you, Maggie?'

14

Maggie downed her glass of whiskey in one gulp, then poured herself another from the bottle. Cole waited, noting the way her eyes shifted nervously, checking the other occupants of the saloon.

At last she said, 'You gonna tell anyone else that?'

'Ain't plannin' to at the moment,' Cole said. 'It's true though, ain't it?'

She nodded. 'Yeah, it's true.'

'Interestin',' Cole said. 'You've only been in Consolation a few months, Roxy tells me, yet you're showin' an interest in somethin' that happened about twenty years ago. Now why's that, I wonder?'

Maggie stared at her glass and made no reply. Cole glanced around, then lowered his voice. 'You send them anonymous notes I've been hearin' about, too?' he asked.

After a moment, Maggie nodded again.

Cole observed her in silence for a full minute, then he said, 'You must have your reasons, Maggie. Probably ain't none of my business, but you sure unleashed a barrel of snakes by sendin' those notes and puttin' that piece in the newspaper. At least two innocent folk have died as a result, it seems to me. I'm thinkin' of the Bowmans.'

'You think I don't know that?' Maggie said, the deep regret in her voice palpable. 'Gotta live with it for the rest of my life.'

The two of them sat drinking for several minutes, saying nothing. Cole was aware of Roxy watching them from the bar. Other folk were drifting back to their homes. Even so, she made no attempt to hurry them.

'Can't remember the name of the town where we first bumped into one another,' Cole said eventually.

'It was Buckland,' Maggie said. 'The Silver Nugget saloon.'

Cole nodded slowly, remembering. 'That's right,' he said. 'But like I said to you before, I know you weren't goin' by the name of Maggie Brown at that time. Now I'm guessin' the change of name when you came to Consolation might have somethin' to do with what we've been talkin' about. Am I right?'

'Yeah,' Maggie said, after a moment.

'Thought so,' Cole said. 'And until a couple of hours ago, I couldn't remember the name you were usin' back in Buckland. Then it came to me, because I overheard Lew Rosen mention it to somebody else in conversation. The name of Duggan. Back in Buckland, you were Maggie Duggan.'

'Lew mentioned that name about me?' Maggie said.

'Not about you, no,' Cole said. 'I didn't hear the whole conversation, but he seemed to be talkin' about somebody else with that name. Some preacher or other. Lived in Consolation some years ago. That make sense to you?'

'Yeah,' Maggie said, reluctance in her

voice. 'He was my grandfather. My ma's pa.'

'Ah,' Cole said. 'So I'm thinkin' your ma comes from around here.'

'Came from,' Maggie corrected. 'She's dead. Died givin' birth to me.'

'And your pa?'

Maggie sighed. 'Guess I'd better tell you it all,' she said. 'Only thing I ask is, don't spread it around.'

'OK,' Cole said.

'My pa was a man called Will Cord,' Maggie said. 'He and my ma weren't married, although from what I've read, they loved one another passionately and he was plannin' to marry her, havin' got her pregnant.'

'Read?' Cole said.

'My ma kept a journal,' she told him. 'I found it some years ago. That's how I know all this.'

'Go on,' Cole said.

'At first, only the two of them knew she was goin' to have a baby. Then, after Will Cord was shot and killed, she told her father. Like you said, he was a preacher. Seems he couldn't face havin' an illegitimate grandchild around, so he sent my ma — her name was Jane — away East, to live with a couple of maiden aunts. It was them who brought me up after my ma died.' Her face became dark with anger. 'They were cruellest women I ever knew, and believe me I've known some pretty brutal women, doin' the kind of work I do. Couldn't wait to get away from the pair of them.'

Cole looked thoughtful. 'Will Cord,' he said. 'Now he was the fella who was shot for killin' Ali Toombs. Wrongly, people are sayin' all of a sudden — including you in that newspaper announcement. Mmm, it's beginnin' to make some sense.'

'Accordin' to my ma's journal, it was old Joe Hayes who persuaded Luther Hickson — that's Ali Toombs's guardian — that Will Cord was Ali's killer. Got him so riled up that he up and shot Will Cord. Or did he? Again, accordin' to my ma's journal, Luther Hickson almost certainly wasn't Will's killer. It was somebody Joe Hayes paid to do the job.'

'So you blame the Hayes family for your not havin' a pa,' Cole said.

'More than that,' Maggie said. 'It broke my ma's heart when Will was killed. You only have to read what she wrote in her journal to know that. Then bein' sent away to have her baby after her pa realized his daughter was gonna have an illegitimate child — a child she was s'posed to get adopted before returnin' to Consolation — well, that made everythin' worse. My ma may've died havin' me, but the way I see it she died of a broken heart, leavin' me to be brought up by the most inhuman women who walked on God's earth! And all that's down to the Hayes family!'

Cole rubbed his chin. 'There's also the fact that Wes and Harry Hayes got away with killin' a poor wretch of a young girl,' he said.

'That, too,' Maggie agreed. 'They're

scum, all of them!'

'They were none too kind to my pa and ma either,' Cole said. And he told her his story, finishing with, 'Like you, I hold Joe Hayes responsible for my parents' death. He as good as murdered them.'

The two of them sat silently. The whiskey bottle was nearly empty and they were the only two customers left in the room. Roxy was polishing glasses that didn't need polishing, allowing her most popular saloon dove to get off her chest whatever it was that needed to be gotten off. She couldn't hear the conversation, but she instinctively knew it was important to both Cole and Maggie, so for that reason she was willing to forgo her sleep.

'So what happens next?' Maggie said. 'I don't want more innocent folk killed.'

'Guess the next move's up to Wes Hayes,' Cole said. 'Or maybe Warren Speer. It's gonna be difficult for him to turn a blind eye to what's happened to Lew Rosen. Folk are beginnin' to turn on the Hayes family.'

'Yeah, and Warren's married to one of them. Wes's daughter, Lucy.'

'So we wait and see, for the moment anyway.' Cole glanced at the clock over the bar. It said ten minutes after three. He stood up and smiled at Maggie. 'Time we let Roxy get her beauty sleep.'

'You stayin' in Consolation?' Maggie asked.

'For the moment,' Cole replied.

'Good,' she said.

15

Three hours earlier, a wide-awake Warren Speer had heard the sound of the dynamite explosion and cringed in his bed. His first instinct was to shove his head under his pillow. Though the noise had been dulled by distance — Warren's house being on the edge of town, like Harry Hayes's place — it had been enough to wake his wife.

'Warren?' she said, rubbing the sleep from her eyes. 'Did I hear something?'

'It was nothing. Go back to sleep, Lucy,' he answered.

Something in his voice made her sit up and look at him. Her eyes were accustomed to the darkness and she could see as well as sense his feeling of panic.

'What is it?' she demanded. 'Something's happened. Something bad, I can tell.'

He got out of bed and began to pull on his clothes in the semi-darkness. 'Go back to sleep,' he said again.

'Not until you tell me,' Lucy said.

Pulling his shirt over his head, he said, 'Reckon Bud will be payin' us a call soon. I need to be ready.'

'Why?' Lucy asked. 'Has something happened in town?'

'It's your damned father!' Warren said, exasperation finally getting the better of his reticence.

Now it was Lucy's turn to feel fearful. 'What's he done now?' she said.

'Probably blown up the *Gazette* office, and Lew Rosen with it!' Warren told her.

'Dear God!' she said.

'Lucy, we need to get out of this town. Get as far from Consolation as we can get. I ain't takin' any more of your pa's orders, or any more of his money, you understand?'

She lit the oil lamp on the table by the bed, her hands shaking as she replaced the glass funnel. Then she stared at her husband and Warren saw the anxiety written all over her face.

He crossed the room and sat on the edge of the bed, putting a consoling arm around her shoulders. He worshipped this girl, would die for her if necessary. Had it not been for her and her misplaced loyalty to her father and grandfather, he would have cleared out of Consolation months ago. Taking on the job of sheriff had been the biggest mistake he had ever made. He should never have allowed himself to be cajoled into it by his pretty little wife and her powerfully persuasive father and his money.

'Maybe — maybe you're wrong, Warren,' she said, shakily. 'Maybe it was just the newspaper office that's been blown up.'

'Lew Rosen lives at the back of the office, remember? And that was a mighty big explosion I just heard. Enough to destroy the whole buildin', maybe set fire to half the street.'

'What will Bud do?'

'He'll come lookin' for me,' Warren said.

And they sat huddled together, waiting.

* * *

After Bud had been to see Zeke Laine and arranged with him to get the remains of Lew Rosen taken to the undertaker's parlour, he headed for Warren Speer's home.

'Can't believe Warren ain't heard nothin',' he muttered to himself as he rode to the edge of town. 'The explosion was enough to wake the dead. Fire lit up half the town afore we got it under control.'

Bud wondered what sort of reception he'd get from the sheriff, particularly when he told him about the two riders from Circle H hightailing it out of town. No question that Wes Hayes or his father was behind the dynamiting of the *Gazette* building. Even Warren would have to admit that.

Bud had been worried about Warren just lately. More and more the sheriff seemed to be ready to surrender to the whims and wishes of Wes Hayes. It just wasn't right. Bud had agreed to be Warren's deputy thinking that he would be helping to enforce the law fairly and impartially. Lately, it seemed he'd been mistaken.

He was only half-surprised to see the light in the upstairs room of Warren's house as he rode up. So the explosion *had* roused Warren and his wife. In which case, why hadn't Warren come to investigate?

Because he had already known about the scheme to blow up Lew and his newspaper office and had no need to come and see what had happened.

The thought refused to leave Bud's mind as he hammered on Warren's front door. The sheriff opened it a minute later. He was fully dressed, Bud noted, his spirits sinking.

'Big trouble, Warren,' he said. 'And you ain't goin' to like it.'

Warren sighed. 'Come in, Bud,' he said.

Bud followed him through into the parlour. He was surprised to see Lucy sitting in one corner of the room, hunched in a deep armchair in her dressing-gown. She was in the half-shadow cast by a lamp, but Bud could see that her face was pale and drawn.

'Howdy, Lucy,' Bud said.

'Hello, Bud,' she replied weakly.

'Take a seat, Bud,' Warren said, nodding towards a chair.

'I won't, if you don't mind,' Bud said. He looked hard at Warren. 'You hear the explosion in town?'

'Thought I heard *somethin*' earlier,' Warren said. 'Somethin' woke me, so if there's been an explosion, I guess that's what it was. You know how it is when you wake up first. You're kinda disoriented.'

'Yeah, sure,' Bud said. 'But you got up and dressed.'

'Yeah,' Warren said. 'Thought I might take a wander into town to see if everythin' was OK. Seems it ain't though, is that right?'

'It sure ain't,' Bud said. 'Lew Rosen is dead. Somebody dynamited the *Gazette* office, set fire to the whole buildin'. Lew died in the fire.'

Lucy whimpered and put a hand to her mouth.

'Gee, that's terrible,' Warren said.

Bud stared at the sheriff and waited. When Warren said nothing, he went on, 'Don't you want to know who did it, Warren?' he said.

'Well, sure!' Warren said. 'You mean, you *know* who did it?'

'Got a pretty good idea. Ed White saw two Circle H men ridin' hell-for-leather outa town just seconds before the explosion.'

Warren licked his lips and glanced at his wife before saying, 'Is Ed sure about that?'

'Sure as he can be. Reckons it was Jim Ellis and Chet Gilman.'

Warren gulped and ran a hand through his hair. 'Oh,' he said.

'What we gonna do?' Bud wanted to know. 'Can't just let it lie.' He looked at Lucy. 'Sorry about this, Lucy, but whichever way you look at it, your pa seems to be implicated.'

'Now hold on, Bud,' Warren said. 'Wes may know nothin' about this. Could be that Lew did somethin' to rile Jim Ellis or Chet Gilman, and they were just takin' their revenge.'

Bud sighed. 'You don't believe that, Warren.'

'Well, listen. I'll ride out to the Circle H at first light. See what Jim and Chet have to say.'

'Better talk to Wes, as well,' Bud said.

'Sure, sure,' Warren said. 'You leave it with me, Bud.'

'Wouldn't you like me to come with you?'

'Nope,' Warren said quickly. 'Best I handle this myself. You get back into town. Try and get some sleep. I'll talk to you later this mornin', OK?'

'OK,' Bud said, reluctantly. ' 'Bye, Lucy.'

''Bye, Bud,' she answered. Her eyes were moist with tears.

★ ★ ★

Warren walked to the door with Bud and watched him ride away before returning to the parlour. Lucy was still curled up in the chair, a look of sheer dread on her face.

Warren sank down in a chair opposite her, with a similarly bleak expression. 'I'll ride out shortly,' he said. 'It's gettin' light, and I need to get this over with.'

'What are you going to do?' she asked.

'Ain't decided.' He looked at her. 'Your pa's gone too far this time, Lucy. It's my bet the town's gonna turn against him. And if that happens, we're best out of this place.'

16

Wes was eating a large breakfast of steak and eggs when his son-in-law arrived. He looked up from the table as his housekeeper came in with the young sheriff.

'I told him you were eatin' your breakfast, Mr Wes,' she said. 'But I couldn't stop — '

'It's all right, Martha,' Wes broke in, looking past her at Warren. 'I've been expectin' him.'

The two men waited until the housekeeper was out of earshot before both speaking at once.

'Wes, I gotta — ' Warren began.

'Coffee, Warren?' Wes said.

Wes smiled. 'Sit down, Warren. You look tuckered out. Like you've been up half the night.'

'I have.' Warren said, slumping into a chair across the table from his father-in-law. 'Got woken up by an explosion in the town.'

Wes nodded. 'So?'

'Lew Rosen's dead. The *Gazette* office is just a heap of ashes.'

Wes took a mouthful of steak and chewed it slowly. At last he said, 'Well, that's tragic. Not that Lew Rosen was ever a friend of the Hayes family, but it's always sad when somebody has to — well, when somebody dies.'

It was too much for Warren. 'Jesus, Wes! You're such a hypocrite. You know damn well the only reason Lew is dead is because of those editorials of his.'

A threatening expression came to Wes's face. 'What you sayin', Warren? That I blew up his office?'

'That you ordered it to be blown up,' Warren said. 'Ain't no good denyin' it. For a start, a witness saw Chet Gilman and Jim Ellis ridin' away fast, just seconds afore the explosion.'

Wes looked thoughtful. 'A witness?'

'Ed White, owner of the hardware store,' Warren said without thinking, then could have bitten his tongue off.

'Ed White,' Wes said the name slowly, as if digesting an unpleasant morsel of food. 'Just the one witness?'

'Yeah, but listen, Wes — '

'No!' Wes barked. 'You listen. You're gonna convince Ed White he was wrong, d'you hear me?'

'Ed ain't gonna be talked outa this, Wes,' Warren warned. 'You might as well accept that. Like a lot of folk in town, Ed's angrier than a hornet.'

'Then he must be silenced,' Wes said, matter-of-factly. 'Deal with it, Warren.' He took another mouthful of steak.

Warren stared at him in silence for several moments, then he took the sheriff's badge from his shirt and tossed it across the table. 'I'm through, Wes,' he said. 'I ain't doin' any more of your dirty work. T'ain't worth it.'

Wes glanced at the badge, then looked up at Warren. 'It ain't?' he said.

'No,' Warren said. 'And another thing, Lucy and I are leavin' Consolation.'

Wes swallowed his mouthful of steak, then took a sip of coffee before speaking.

'You ain't takin' my daughter anywhere, Warren. For one thing, she'll never agree, and — '

'She already has,' Warren informed him.

'What!'

'We're leavin', Wes,' Warren said. 'Ain't a thing you can do about it.'

Wes scowled at him. 'Don't be too sure about that,' he said. 'Now get out!'

He waited until Warren had left the room before pushing his plate away, his appetite having suddenly deserted him. After a few minutes, he opened a window and shouted across to a man emerging from the bunkhouse.

'Tex! Get over here!'

The man was a tall, lanky individual with a hatchet-shaped face and a loping gait. He ambled across to the open window, in no particular hurry. An impatient Wes drummed his fingers on the window ledge.

'Yeah, boss?' Tex said.

'Got a little tidyin'-up job for you and Joe McCain to do in town,' Wes told him. 'And I want it done fast. There's a man called Ed White, he owns the hardware store . . . '

* * *

Warren rode back to town like a man who has off-loaded a huge weight from his shoulders. Whilst being a mite apprehensive about his and Lucy's future, he felt optimistic for the first time in months. Dammit, he'd been a fool ever to get under the thumb of a man like Wes Hayes, he told himself.

Getting away from Consolation would be a chance for him and Lucy to make a fresh start. They had a little money saved, and he'd find work somewhere, somehow. Any job except lawman, he'd had enough of that. He rode in a leisurely fashion, turning these thoughts over in his mind, preoccupied to such an extent that he was only aware of two other riders after they had passed him on the trail.

He didn't see their faces, but something about their rear-view shape and bearing seemed familiar. One thing was plain, they were in a hurry to get somewhere.

Warren stopped at a creek to allow his mare to take a drink and for himself to freshen-up before going on. So it was another hour before he finally arrived back in Consolation. He rode directly to the sheriff's office, gradually becoming conscious of little groups of folk dotted along the street, all talking animatedly about something.

He was tethering his horse to the hitching rail when Bud came out to meet him on the boardwalk.

'Got some bad news,' Bud said, before Warren had a chance to speak. 'Ed White's dead.'

Warren's stomach seemed to turn a somersault. 'What!' he said. 'When? How did it happen?'

''Bout half an hour ago,' Bud said.

'Coupla guys, bandannas over their faces, burst into the hardware store, pumped half-a-dozen bullets into Ed, who was behind the counter, and scarpered. Rosie Matlan was in the store at the time. Fainted clear away as soon as the first shot was fired.'

'Dear God!' Warren said.

'Weren't no robbery, either. The two men took nothin'. Plain premeditated murder, Warren, that's what it was. Sophie White was in the room at the back of the store. She heard the shots and came runnin', but she was too late to see anythin' except the backs of the two critters as they rode off.'

It was at this point that Bud noticed Warren wasn't wearing his tin badge.

'Warren? Where's your badge?'

Warren wiped the sweat from his brow with his shirtsleeve. He looked and felt sick.

'I quit,' he told Bud. 'Left my badge on Wes Hayes's table. Guess that puts you in charge of things, Bud.'

'Me?' Bud said, alarmed. 'Hold on a

minute, I ain't ready to be no sheriff.'

'Me neither, not in this town,' Warren said. 'Sorry, Bud, you're gonna have to take over until Consolation can find itself another sheriff.'

With that, he unhitched his mare and mounted. Bud watched open-mouthed as he rode away.

★ ★ ★

Cole saw Warren riding away from the sheriff's office as he emerged from the hotel. He had planned to go to Roxy's Palace to check on Maggie, but changed direction when he saw the shocked expression on Bud Randall's face as he, too, watched the sheriff ride off.

'Somethin' wrong, Bud?' Cole said.

'Sure is, Mr Chance,' Bud said. 'Warren just quit as sheriff, and Ed White's been murdered.'

'Ed White? Ain't he the fella who saw the two riders hightailin' it outa town last night?'

'The same,' Bud said. 'So now there ain't no witnesses, just hearsay. Maybe it was the same two fellas who've shot and killed Ed.'

'Maybe,' Cole said. 'Anybody been to see Wes Hayes about the explosion at the newspaper office?'

'Warren went out early this morning at first light. Reckon he stayed just long enough to tell Wes he was quittin' his job.'

'And almost certainly to tell him what Ed White saw last night,' Cole said, thoughtfully. 'It's the only explanation for the prompt attack on Ed at his store. Wes would have given orders for Ed's killin' the minute Warren left the Circle H.' He stared at the young deputy and smiled. 'You're lookin' a little green about the gills, Bud.'

'I ain't up to this, Mr. Chance. What we need here is a professional lawman, a marshal or some such.'

'Take too long,' Cole said. 'We need to act fast, tackle Wes Hayes head on. The way things are goin', this whole town's gonna belong to him soon. Anybody opposes him, he just gets his gunslingers to wipe 'em out. Folk are gonna be afraid to move or speak out for fear of upsettin' him.'

'You said 'we need to act fast', Mr Chance,' Bud said, a hopeful look in his eye. 'That mean you're prepared to help?'

Cole shrugged. 'Guess I am.'

'That's swell,' Bud said. 'Sure can use the help of somebody like you. What d'you reckon we should do first?'

'Get some of the townsmen together. Men you think might be prepared to confront Wes Hayes and his gunslingers. Men who ain't afraid to use a gun. Then we go out to the Circle H and you're gonna arrest Chet Gilman and Jim Ellis. A whole heap of folk heard Ed White's statement about the two of them ridin' away just before the explosion. OK, it may just be hearsay evidence, but it's a start.'

'Sure thing, Mr Chance,' Bud said. 'I'll get started with Vince Chessman and a few others who've had their businesses taken away by Wes and Harry Hayes. Reckon they'll back us.'

'We'll meet up in an hour at Roxy's Palace,' Cole said.

17

At the same time as Warren was tethering his mare outside the sheriff's office in Consolation, Joe Hayes was entering his son's study at the Circle H, leaning heavily on a silver-topped cane.

The pain in Joe's gut was huge. No amount of drugs prescribed to him by Doc Tully seemed to be having any effect now, and his breathing was restricted to short painful gasps. Even so, he had gathered up sufficient strength to come and confront his remaining son.

'Pa,' Wes said, looking up from the papers on his desk. 'Why ain't you in bed? Martha said you was extra poorly this mornin'.'

'I was, and I am,' Joe gasped.

He collapsed in the chair opposite his son. A fierce sun shone through the window behind Wes, and Joe had to shield his eyes. Wes, noting this, turned and pulled down the blind.

'Tell me what's goin' on, Wes,' Joe said, fighting for breath. 'I want to know *all* of it. Don't go shieldin' me from anythin'.'

Wes sighed. 'OK, Pa.' He recognized the uncompromising look in the old man's eye and knew he had to come clean. 'You know Harry is dead,' he began.

'I do,' Joe said, his grief plain to see. 'No thanks to you, Wes. Had to hear it from one of the men. Seems he had a fight with Tom Bowman, then died of a heart attack.'

Wes nodded, then began by telling him about Tom and Lily Bowman's death — his version of Tom's accidental shooting of Lily followed by Tom's suicide. He tried to ignore the sceptical look on his father's face as he recounted this story.

Wes then went on to tell Joe about the 'necessary destruction' of the *Gazette* office and Lew Rosen's 'unfortunate' death, Warren's resignation as sheriff, and finally the 'unavoidable' killing of Ed White.

Joe Hayes was no fool, he could read between the lines. Neither was he squeamish. Years ago, when times were different and folks settled their own disputes and disagreements, more often than not violently, he might have done something similar to get rid of Lew Rosen and his poisonous editorials. But that was then and this was now. He'd grown older and wiser, and he knew for a fact that Lew Rosen had been a popular and influential member of Consolation's community. Folks were not going to take kindly to the manner of his death. It spelled trouble, whichever way you looked at it.

'What about . . . ' — he took some painful breaths before going on — 'the Ali Toombs business? The notes?'

'They've stopped since Harry died.' Wes told him.

'D'you reckon Lew Rosen . . . ?' Joe was unable to finish the sentence.

Wes shook his head. 'No, Lew never

sent them. Nor did he write that announcement in the *Gazette*. At first I thought he was guilty on both counts, but now I'm sure he wasn't.'

'So who . . . ?'

'Cole Chance is my bet,' Wes said.

'He still around?'

'Last I heard, he was,' Wes said. 'He's trouble, in more ways than one.'

'So, what're you gonna do about him?'

Wes shrugged nonchalantly. 'Kill him, I guess.'

Joe put his head in his hands. 'Sweet Jesus, how did it come to this?' he muttered.

★　★　★

Cole left Bud to assemble a group of men willing to confront Wes Hayes, and possibly old Joe Hayes, and went on to Roxy's Palace.

It was mid-morning, and the saloon was empty of customers except for two old-timers sitting at a table playing dominoes, each nursing a glass of beer. They glanced up as Cole entered, then resumed their game.

Roxy was talking with the barkeep, behind the bar. When she saw Cole, she moved towards him.

'Get you a drink?' she enquired.

Cole shook his head. 'I came to see Maggie.'

'She's in her room,' Roxy said. Then, seeing Cole's raised eyebrow, added, 'No, there's nobody with her. Go on up, if you like.'

'OK,' Cole said.

'You two are pretty friendly,' Roxy observed. '*Old* friends?'

'Not really. We just know each other from some other place.'

'She's a fine girl, Maggie is,' Roxy said. 'Thinkin' of makin' her a partner in this business. One thing's certain, she's too damn good for whorin' and puttin' up with the likes of Wes Hayes.' She looked hard at Cole. 'Reckon she needs a friend, right now. Seems she's got somethin' on her mind. What — ?'

Cole turned towards the staircase, deliberately cutting off any further questions. As he did so, he saw Maggie descending. He caught her eye and nodded towards a corner table where they were unlikely to be overheard.

'What's happenin'?' she asked him, when they were sitting together. 'I saw Bud Randall from my window. He seems to be goin' round gatherin' up a posse. Has something else happened?'

Cole shook his head. 'It's not exactly a posse. Just some fellas to ride out with us when we go and see Wes Hayes. Strength in numbers, and all that. We're meetin' here in an hour.'

'You're goin' to see Wes?' she said. She glanced at the clock above the bar. 'He'll probably be here to see me in another half-hour. You can save yourself the journey.'

Cole looked at her thoughtfully. 'You ain't got any qualms about . . . entertainin' him, then?'

She shrugged. 'It's what I do.' She glanced at Roxy. 'It's what I'm *paid* to do. Don't have to like it, though.'

'About the anonymous notes,' Cole began.

Maggie shook her head. 'They're finished. Ain't gonna write any more. Harry was the only member of the Hayes family likely to be rattled by them and goaded into doin' somethin' stupid, and he's dead. And there's no newspaper to put any more announcements in. Guess I'll have to think of some other way of gettin' folk to think about the Ali Toombs business afresh and realize the Hayes boys were her killers.'

'What was your reasonin' behind the notes?' Cole asked. 'To bring the Hayes family down? 'Cause that looks close to happenin' now. Wes went a step too far blowin' up the *Gazette* office and killin' Lew Rosen. Lew was well liked hereabouts.'

Maggie was about to reply when they became aware of a sudden hub-bub of voices and movement out in the street.

'Somethin's happenin',' she said.

They both got up and hurried towards the batwings. Roxy and the barkeep joined them, followed by the two old-timers.

18

The scene that greeted Cole was one of confrontation. A half-circle of towns-men had gathered in the centre of the street. They were facing Wes Hayes and three of the Circle H men, all of whom were on horses. Jim Ellis and Chet Gilman were two of the men. Cole didn't know the other.

Bud Randall was standing in the centre of the semi-circle, slightly in front of the crowd. He was looking up at Wes Hayes who had a wry grin on his face.

'So you reckon you're sheriff now, Bud,' Wes was saying.

'Nope,' Bud said. 'Still a deputy, but the law here until somebody else takes over, Mr Hayes.'

Wes nodded, then glanced towards the saloon, catching sight of Cole and Maggie on the boardwalk outside.

'Then your first job had better be to arrest Cole Chance. He's a wanted man with a price on his head.'

'Nope,' Bud said. He pointed at Chet Gilman and Jim Ellis. 'My first job is to arrest those two *hombres* for blowin' up the *Gazette* office and killin' Lew Rosen.'

Wes seemed unmoved, as did the two men mentioned. 'You got any evidence to back that up?' Wes asked. 'You got a witness?'

'You know damn well I ain't,' Bud said. 'Coupla men shot and killed Ed White earlier this mornin'. But a lot of folk here heard what he said last night, and Ed was positive it was Chet Gilman and Jim Ellis who did the dynamitin'.'

'Hearsay,' Wes said. 'Ain't proof. So don't try layin' a hand on my men or you'll have to face the consequences, Bud.'

To emphasize the point, the three Circle H men rested their hands on their sidearms.

'You seen how many men I got

standin' behind me?' Bud said. 'And all are armed.'

Wes looked unperturbed. 'Sure,' he said. 'But a lot of 'em are gonna die if they try usin' those guns.'

'And you'll be the first, Hayes,' Cole said from the boardwalk, his .45 Peacemaker already in his hand.

Wes stared at him for a moment, then dismounted from his horse and walked slowly towards the saloon.

'Wait for me, fellas,' he said over his shoulder. 'Mister Chance and I have some talkin' to do afore anybody does any arrestin'. And you hold your horses, *Deputy* Randall. No sense causin' bloodshed if it can be avoided.'

He brushed past Cole and walked on into the saloon, leaving an uneasy situation in the street. Bud, for one, seemed doubtful about what to do.

Cole holstered his .45. 'Leave it for the moment, Bud,' he said, then turned and went into the saloon.

Maggie followed him. Roxy and the barkeep, who had already retreated into the saloon, positioned themselves behind the bar. The two old-timers beat a hasty retreat out of a back door.

Wes walked across and leaned on the bar. Without a word, the barkeep took a bottle and a glass from the shelf behind him and placed both in front of Wes. After a glance at Cole, he took another glass and pushed it towards him.

'You want a drink, Maggie?' Wes asked.

'No, thanks,' Maggie said. She positioned herself beside Cole.

Wes looked Maggie up and down, as if examining a piece of prime beef.

'Interestin',' he said. 'I see you've taken sides, Maggie.' He smiled, but there was no humour in it. 'Big mistake.'

'Say what you've got to say, Hayes,' Cole said.

The other man poured himself a drink, then raised a questioning eyebrow at Cole, who shook his head.

'The notes sent to Harry,' Wes said, after taking a swig of his whiskey. 'Reckon they killed him, indirectly, don't you?'

'Maybe,' Cole said.

'Ah!' Wes pounced. 'So you' ain't denyin' you sent 'em?'

Cole made no reply.

'Harry got the crazy idea that Tom Bowman was behind 'em,' Wes went on. 'That's how he came to go out there and pick a fight with Bowman. Ended up killin' himself.' He looked at Cole thoughtfully. 'Why'd you send 'em? What is it you reckon you know about Ali Toombs's death? Far as I remember, you'd left the territory by the time she died.'

'Cole didn't send the notes, I did,' Maggie said, her voice shaking.

A look of astonishment spread across Wes's face as he turned to stare at her. The look turned to one of fury. '*You?*'

'Me,' Maggie said, defiantly.

'Why?' he demanded. 'Why in hell do you care who killed some girl twenty years ago? You, a cheap whore!'

Maggie gave a rueful smile. 'Yeah, that's me, a cheap whore. 'Cept things might've been different if my ma and pa had lived.'

'What's you're ma and pa got to do with all this?' Wes asked.

'Will Cord was my father,' Maggie told him. 'Jane Duggan was my mother. Remember her? She was the preacher's daughter.'

Wes stared at her. 'Sure, I remember,' he said, after a moment.

'Your father arranged to have Will Cord murdered, and for him to take the blame for a killin' you and your brother were responsible for,' Maggie went on, her voice becoming stronger by the second. 'My ma was pregnant with me at the time, and Will Cord was goin' to marry her. Instead of that, her pa sent her away, and she died givin' birth to me. Died with a broken heart. Because of your poisonous family, Wes, I never knew my mother.'

Wes continued to stare at her. He seemed at a loss for words. But before Maggie could go on, they heard the first rumblings of a commotion outside. It seemed the crowd's patience was running out.

Wes, Cole and Maggie hurried to the batwings, just in time to see Vince Chessman lift his Winchester and fire a shot at Jim Ellis. 'That's for my pal, Lew, you bastard!' he yelled.

The shot caught Ellis on the shoulder, but he was still able to return fire. Seconds later, a spurt of blood exploded from Vince's midriff and he fell back into the arms of the men behind him.

It was the signal for all hell to break loose as guns opened up in a roar of flying lead and flame.

The crowd of townsmen scattered, two men dragging Vince to the Horseshoe, others diving for whatever cover they could find. The three Circle H men began firing indiscriminately, their startled horses bucking and wheeling. One of the men's bullets scorched the side of Bud Randall's cheek as he scrambled behind the water trough outside the barbershop. Max Prentiss caught a bullet in the back as he ran for the boardwalk outside the hardware store. The slug threw him forward on his face where he lay without moving. Another townsman fell in a splurge of blood and brains as Chet Gilman's shot tore open the back of his head.

Seconds later, Chet Gilman himself screamed and was spun from his horse, one bullet from Cole's .45 tearing through his neck, another ploughing into his chest.

The third man turned and began riding away fast through thickening clouds of gunsmoke. A bullet winged him on the left leg, but he kept going until a second bullet — this one from Bud Randall's Winchester — brought him down, his foot catching in his stirrup so that his sprawled body was dragged along behind his fleeing horse.

Jim Ellis continued putting up a fight until a profusion of bullets from several directions ploughed into him, lead biting deep into all parts of his head and torso, sending him crashing to the ground.

Unbeknown to Cole, Wes Hayes had used the distraction of the street battle to grab Maggie and pull her back into the saloon. By the time Cole pushed throught the batwings, his Peacemaker drawn, Wes had her pressed against him, an arm round her neck and his .45 jammed against her forehead.

'Stay where you are, or I'll kill her!' he yelled at Cole. 'And drop your gun!'

Cole sighed and dropped the .45, trying to ignore Maggie's terrified face. 'You're through, Hayes,' he said. 'There ain't no way outa this for you. Let her go and come quietly.'

Wes gave a barking laugh. 'Are you kiddin'? Maggie's my ticket outa here. And when my pa hears what's happened — '

'Your pa's dyin',' Cole cut in. 'T'ain't no use tryin' to hide behind him any more. Same thing with the rest of those gunslingers of yours, when they hear what happened to Jim, Chet and that other fella you brought with you. Think they're gonna hang around? Well, they ain't. The whole town's against you, Hayes. You're finished.'

'You reckon?' Wes said, a crazed look in his eyes. 'I'll die first, and this bitch'll die with me!'

'No!' Maggie screamed, struggling. 'Please!'

Powerless to help her, Cole used the only tactic he could think of: to keep Wes talking until he could think of a way out of the situation.

'So you're gonna kill another young woman, are you, Wes?' he said. 'First Ali Toombs, now Maggie.' He rubbed a palm across his chin. 'Or maybe Ali Toombs's death was an accident. Maybe you and Harry didn't really mean to kill her. Is that what happened, Wes? Did things just get outa hand? Maybe you were a little rough and — '

'Shut up!' Wes broke in, eyes blazing, spittle at the sides of his mouth. 'Yeah, all right, we roughed her up a little. But then the little bitch threatened to run and tell folks how we'd held her down and done it to her. Threatened to boast about it! Harry panicked. Nigh on went loco. Beat her about the face, then put his hands round her throat. Dammit, he'd choked her to death before I could stop him!' He noticed the scepticism in Cole's face. 'Difficult to believe, ain't it, but it's true? Harry was a different person in those days. Real evil when he got mad. But somehow, when the realization of what he'd done sunk in, he kinda went to pieces. Never was the same again.'

As Wes was speaking, Roxy moved slowly, quietly along behind the bar. Not daring to breathe, she reached under it, and eased out the Winchester that she kept there in readiness for any trouble. Her hands were shaking and her fringe of bleached-blonde hair was sticking to the cold lather of sweat on her forehead.

'But enough talkin',' Wes was saying. 'Time I was gettin' outa here.' Maintaining the grip around Maggie's neck, he moved his gun from her forehead and turned it towards Cole. 'But first off, I'm gonna kill you, Mister Ex-Gun-slinger. Seems to me you've gotta lot to answer for, stirrin' folks up to act against me.'

Cole breathed steadily but said nothing, his eyes bright with defiance.

Wes grimaced. 'Never did like you or your folks. And I don't — '

It was as far as he got before Roxy gritted her teeth and fired the Winchester. Her aim in her shaking hands was poor and the bullet only grazed Wes's head, but it was sufficient to make him turn and drop his arm from around Maggie. As she ran towards the bar, Cole threw himself to the floor, snatching up his .45 and firing it at Wes in one smooth movement.

The bullet entered Wes's head through his right ear, throwing him sideways across the table at which the two old-timers had been playing dominoes. The domino tiles flew across the room as the table splintered under Wes's dead weight.

For a moment, nobody moved. Then Roxy came from behind the bar and put a comforting arm around Maggie, who was shaking and whimpering.

'Take it easy, girl,' Roxy said. 'It's all over. Wes Hayes ain't gonna hurt you any more. Ain't gonna hurt anybody any more.'

She glanced at Cole who had got to his feet and was looking at the body. At the same moment, Bud Randall came through the batwings, followed by a small group of townsmen and Nettie Garland. Nettie seemed to have aged visibly since hearing about Lew Rosen's death.

Bud walked across to join Cole and looked down at Wes.

'He dead?' Bud asked.

Cole nodded. 'How are things outside? Many hurt?'

'Vince Chessman's pretty bad, but he'll live,' Bud said. 'The doc's with him now. Max Prentiss and Ted Fear are dead. Two other fellas got winged, but nothin' serious.' He gestured towards Wes. 'What're we gonna do about him?'

243

Cole thought for a moment. 'We should take him back to his pa,' he said eventually.

'Yeah, maybe you're right,' Bud agreed.

19

When Wes and the other Circle H men hadn't returned from town by dawn, Joe Hayes began to prepare himself for news of the worst kind. He knew it was only a matter of time before the lifeless body of his second son would be brought to him.

Two sons dead.

A feeling of immense loneliness and gut-wrenching despair swept over him, as he sat waiting for news. If, as he suspected, Wes was dead, what was left for him? More land than a sick man could cope with. A bank, a hotel, a saloon. And a clutch of small businesses obtained by his two unscrupulous sons, businesses in which Joe had no interest whatsoever.

One glimmer of light amongst all the gloom. He still had Bella, his fourteen-year-old granddaughter. When he died, as he surely would in a few months' time, everything he owned would be hers. But would she want it? Somehow he didn't think so. She was a bright, intelligent girl who took after her mother, and she'd talked to her father about wanting to go to college. Harry had stalled, aware that she was too valuable to him as his housekeeper, but Joe knew his son had planned to let her go when he'd married the rich widow from Chicago. So maybe he could put money in trust for Bella, and send her East to college. It would be something positive. What else?

Old habits died hard. After a lifetime of planning and scheming, calculating and plotting, Joe found himself — even in these moments of deep anguish — weighing up and listing possibilities. Things he could maybe do to undo some of the Wes and Harry's transgressions.

Sell most of the land, or give it back to the homesteaders and farmers who'd once owned it.

Sell the small businesses, or maybe give them back to the people who had once run them before their mortgages had been foreclosed or their loans cancelled.

Write off any other loans or mortgages owed by local people. He could well afford it.

Let First National buy up the bank — they'd approached him and Harry about it often enough.

Sell the hotel and the Horseshoe saloon.

Did he have enough time left to do these things?

★ ★ ★

Joe saw the buckboard coming through a veil of early morning mist as he stood watching and waiting on the veranda outside the ranch house. One man drove the buckboard and another rode alongside, but it was some minutes more before Joe could identify Bud Randall as the driver, and Cole Chance

247

sitting high in the saddle of the sorrel.

By the time the buckboard and the rider reached the house, a bunch of Circle H hands had emerged from the bunkhouse to witness the return of their boss, sensing catastrophe. Joe knew the men had long since considered him nothing more than a figurehead at the Circle H, so they would be apprehensive about their future.

He crossed his arms and forced himself to stand erect, ignoring the pain in his gut and the pounding behind his eyes. He watched Cole dismount and Bud ease himself down from the buckboard, and tried not to look at the blanket-covered shape in the back of the conveyance.

* * *

At the same time as Cole and Bud were arriving at the Circle H, Maggie was soaking in a tub in a back room at Roxy's Palace. It had been Roxy's suggestion in an effort to relax the girl after the harrowing events of the night.

And it seemed to be having the calming effect the saloon owner had hoped for. The lines of anxiety in Maggie's features had perceptively softened.

Roxy sat on a stool next to the tub.

'I'm gonna make a few changes around here,' she told Maggie. 'I'm gettin' too old to run this place singlehanded; what I need is a pardner. Somebody younger, with the kinda energy I had when I was your age. Whadda y'say?'

Maggie dropped the soap in the water and stared at her. 'You askin' *me* to be your pardner?'

'Sure I am,' Roxy said. She frowned. 'Of course, you might be hopin' for a better offer from that Chance fella. Seems he's taken a shine to you.'

Maggie shook her head. 'Nope, settlin' down ain't for me, and I don't reckon it is for Cole either. At least, not yet awhile.'

'Yeah, maybe you're right,' Roxy agreed.

Maggie heaved herself out of the tub

and Roxy tossed her a towel.

'So, whadda y'say?' Roxy asked again. 'Pardner?'

Maggie smiled. 'Pardner!' she said.

★ ★ ★

Two days later, Cole rode out of Consolation without any clear idea of where he was heading. Sufficient to know that he'd made the right decision. For a brief moment or two, he'd thought of clearing Tom Bowman's bank loan and taking over Tom's homestead. Maybe asking Maggie to join him . . .

But it hadn't taken him long to dismiss the idea. For one thing, Maggie was no homesteader, never would be. For another, Roxy had told him she'd made Maggie her partner in the saloon. Probably the best thing that could have happened to the girl.

Also, if truth were told, he wasn't ready to settle anywhere just yet. He had a tad more brooding to do, a mite

250

more heart-searching.

'You sure left a big hole in my life, Louise,' he muttered to himself, as he and the sorrel took the trail out of town. 'Ain't found a way of fillin' it yet.'

A few of the townspeople had wanted Cole to stay and take on Warren Speer's job of sheriff, but he had refused. He'd told them they had a ready-made sheriff right there — in Bud Randall. Bud, he'd said, may be young, but he was honest, conscientious and gutsy, everything a town could want in their lawman.

Bud had been hesitant at first, but when he'd seen support for Cole's suggestion swelling amongst the townsfolk, he'd accepted the challenge.

'Reckon I did the right thing, Louise,' Cole muttered. 'Reckon it's what you would've wanted me to do. And somehow — ain't sure how — you'll let me know when it's time for me to settle again.' He chuckled. 'You always did know me better'n I knew myself. It's a funny thing about some women . . . .'

We do hope that you have enjoyed reading this large print book.

Did you know that all of our titles are available for purchase?

We publish a wide range of high quality large print books including:
Romances, Mysteries, Classics
General Fiction
Non Fiction and Westerns

Special interest titles available in large print are:
The Little Oxford Dictionary
Music Book, Song Book
Hymn Book, Service Book

Also available from us courtesy of Oxford University Press:
Young Readers' Dictionary
(large print edition)
Young Readers' Thesaurus
(large print edition)

For further information or a free brochure, please contact us at:
Ulverscroft Large Print Books Ltd.,
The Green, Bradgate Road, Anstey,
Leicester, LE7 7FU, England.
Tel: (00 44) **0116 236 4325**
Fax: (00 44) **0116 234 0205**

Other titles in the
Linford Western Library:

THE JUDAS METAL

Gillian F. Taylor

Pat Williams and Robson Hyde were a successful partnership: they'd gained control of a silver mine down in south-west Texas, but when bandits began to ambush the loads of silver bullion, things changed. It appeared that the bandits had inside information. Who was behind the attacks? A resentful enemy sowed the seeds of doubt in Williams' mind. Did Hyde want all the silver for himself? Suspicion severely tested the pair's friendship, amid several violent deaths at the silver mine.

TWO GUN MARSHAL

John Saunders

Packing two guns, Jeff Bellamy comes to Red Rock to help his father's best friend, but finds Dorlen beyond help, and a town dying because its freight lines are being ruined. Tough man Bellamy dislikes small-timers being pushed around, so he stays. And, when the crooked marshal drops to a well-aimed bullet, takes over his job. But Red Rock comes perilously closer to its demise before its new marshal gets to grips with the instigator of all the trouble.

HIGH MOUNTAIN STAND-OFF

John C. Danner

The only thing Sam Harper knew about himself was his skill with a gun. His past was a blank, his future unknown. Then he met the beautiful and wealthy Virginia Maitland whose life was under threat from unseen enemies — she desperately needed his help to find answers. Together they rode a dangerous trail, battling the raging elements as well as their would-be assassins. Only the crash of gunfire would determine the outcome in a final showdown.

MISFIT LIL CHEATS THE HANGROPE

Chap O'Keefe

Misfit Lil was riding for a fall. She'd chosen to intervene in the fortunes of a wagon train of emigrants, incompetently led by erstwhile outlaw, Luke Reiner, their guide. Lil's first mistake was to save a bunch of children when the wagons were caught in a blizzard, then to enlist Jackson Farraday's assistance. This only resulted in a bloody fight with Reiner. Lil's interventions have serious consequences when Jackson is accused of murder. Can she save him from hanging?

TIME TO KILL

Lee Lejeune

Ten years after the Civil War, ex Confederate soldier Nat Jordan returns by railroad to his home near Kansas City. But so-called Quantrill raiders hold up the train. Their leader, Captain Coulter, recognises Jordan as a fellow Confederate, which leads to complications. Pinkerton agent McGill suspects Nat is in cahoots with the raiders, and tragedy strikes at the Jordan homestead. Who actually is on the side of the law? Because it's time to kill, but who will die?

THE TARNISHED STAR

Jack Martin

Sheriff Cole Masters just wants to raise a family with the woman he loves. But upholding the law, when guns rule, is a dangerous business. When Cole arrests a rancher's son for the murder of a saloon girl, the father will do anything to free his son. And soon the lawman is on the run for murder — chased by two gunmen. The rancher wants Masters dead — but blood will run as Cole Masters attempts to reclaim his tarnished star.